ONE WRONG MOVE AND YOU'RE A DEAD MAN!

Longarm jumped down onto a trail below the ledge and, hugging the mountainside, scuttled back into the rock.

With him out of sight, the firing ceased. But that would not last. The two riflemen had him bracketed and were now just waiting for him to move his ass out of the hole he had just crawled into so they could finish him off. Longarm was fuming. Those two on the trace had not bothered to follow him into the badlands because they had known where he was heading. So they had gone ahead and set up this neat little trap.

And he had walked right into it.

Also in the LONGARM series from Jove

LONGARM
LONGARM AND THE LONE STAR LEGEND
LONGARM AND THE LONE STAR BOUNTY
LONGARM AND THE LONE STAR RUSTLERS
LONGARM AND THE LONE STAR DELIVERANCE
LONGARM IN THE TEXAS PANHANDLE
LONGARM AND THE RANCHER'S SHOWDOWN
LONGARM ON THE INLAND PASSAGE
LONGARM IN THE RUBY RANGE COUNTRY
LONGARM AND THE GREAT CATTLE KILL
LONGARM AND THE CROOKED RAILMAN
LONGARM ON THE SIWASH TRAIL
LONGARM AND THE RUNAWAY THIEVES
LONGARM AND THE ESCAPE ARTIST
LONGARM IN THE BIG BURNOUT
LONGARM AND THE TREACHEROUS TRIAL
LONGARM AND THE NEW MEXICO SHOOT-OUT
LONGARM AND THE LONE STAR FRAME
LONGARM AND THE RENEGADE SERGEANT
LONGARM IN THE SIERRA MADRES
LONGARM AND THE MEDICINE WOLF
LONGARM AND THE INDIAN RAIDERS
LONGARM IN A DESERT SHOWDOWN
LONGARM AND THE REBEL KILLERS
LONGARM AND THE HANGMAN'S LIST
LONGARM IN THE CLEARWATERS
LONGARM AND THE REDWOOD RAIDERS
LONGARM AND THE DEADLY JAILBREAK
LONGARM AND THE PAWNEE KID
LONGARM AND THE DEVIL'S STAGECOACH
LONGARM AND THE WYOMING BLOODBATH
LONGARM IN THE RED DESERT
LONGARM AND THE CROOKED MARSHAL
LONGARM AND THE TEXAS RANGERS
LONGARM AND THE VIGILANTES
LONGARM IN THE OSAGE STRIP
LONGARM AND THE LOST MINE
LONGARM AND THE LONGLEY LEGEND
LONGARM AND THE DEAD MAN'S BADGE
LONGARM AND THE KILLER'S SHADOW
LONGARM AND THE MONTANA MASSACRE
LONGARM IN THE MEXICAN BADLANDS
LONGARM AND THE BOUNTY HUNTRESS
LONGARM AND THE DENVER BUSTOUT
LONGARM AND THE SKULL CANYON GANG
LONGARM AND THE RAILROAD TO HELL
LONGARM AND THE LONESTAR CAPTIVE
LONGARM AND THE RIVER OF DEATH
LONGARM AND THE GOLD HUNTERS
LONGARM AND THE COLORADO GUNDOWN

JOVE BOOKS, NEW YORK

LONGARM AND THE GRAVE ROBBERS

A Jove Book / published by arrangement with
the author

PRINTING HISTORY
Jove edition / November 1991

ISBN: 0-515-10708-5

Jove Books are published by The Berkley Publishing Group,
200 Madison Avenue, New York, New York 10016.
The name "JOVE" and the "J" logo
are trademarks belonging to Jove Publications, Inc.

PRINTED IN THE UNITED STATES OF AMERICA

10 9 8 7 6 5 4 3 2 1

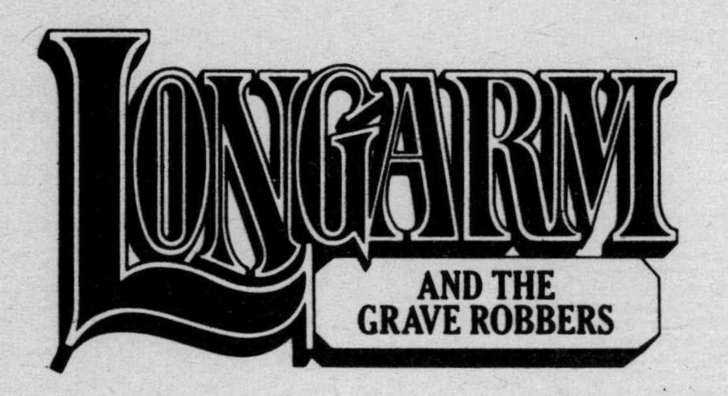
LONGARM
AND THE
GRAVE ROBBERS

Chapter 1

"Grave robbing?" Longarm asked. "For ransom?"

"You know a better reason?" Vail asked.

Longarm shook his head, then unwrapped a cheroot. "I wouldn't figure that—not out here. Not in Golden."

Marshal Billy Vail shrugged, his round, cherubic face somber. "It can happen anywhere, Longarm. And there's enough wealth still in Golden to bring in them vultures."

Longarm lit his cheroot and leaned back in the high-backed leather chair. They were in Marshal Billy Vail's office, the banjo clock on the wall ticking calmly. It was only a little past eight o'clock. For probably the second time in his misspent life, Longarm had arrived at Vail's office on time—only to find Billy as anxious as a cat locked out on a rainy night.

"I thought you were goin' to quit smokin' them weeds," Vail said.

"Hell, chief, this is only my second smoke in two days."

"So why does the second one have to be in here? You know I'm tryin' to quit myself."

"You want me to stub it out?"

Vail waved his hand impatiently. "Let's get to the business at hand, and pretty damn unpleasant business it is, I don't need to tell you. Robbing a grave, then making the grievin' survivors pay a ransom to get their loved one's remains back."

"Yeah," agreed Longarm. "That's a pretty mean trick, all right. But look at it this way. The man's dead. His kin are done grieving. And it ain't as if anything really bad could happen to the corpse now. He's already worm bait. Ain't nothing can change that."

Vail frowned intently at Longarm, his near-pink face getting a mite redder than usual. Then he shook his head in exasperation. "You're a hard man, Custis. Don't you have no consideration at all for the feeling of the grievin' widow at a time like this. Don't you realize what a terrible desecration it is to kidnap her dear departed loved one's corpse so as to make her pay to get it back. It is a cruel and vicious racket."

Longarm could see that Vail was in no mood for levity on the matter. And come to think of it, neither was he. Like Vail, Longarm remembered the awful uproar some years past when kidnappers took Lincoln's corpse and held it for ransom. When they caught the bastards responsible and buried Lincoln's remains a second time, they interred the casket in fresh-poured concrete. Vail was right. It was a crime that should not be taken lightly.

"I agree with you, Billy. It is a cruel and vicious racket."

"Good. Because I'm sending you out to Golden to bring in the bastard who stole the body of my good old buddy Long Tom Sanders."

"Slow down and drive that buggy past me once again, chief. Who the hell is this Tom Sanders?"

"An ol' trail buddy of mine. When we was both young and full of piss and vinegar, we joined up with the Texas Rangers and chased them Comanches over hell and beyond. He saved my hide on more than one occasion, I don't mind admitting—and I returned the favor a couple of times myself. After he left Texas, he joined the army and rode awhile with Zach Taylor; and when he left the army after the Mexican unpleasantness, he came to ground in Golden, made himself a nice pot in the mines before they ran out. But he had a real tight fist, God bless 'im, and left his widow a nice bundle."

"And now his body's been kidnapped."

"That's what happened, all right. He died a month ago and I was at the funeral, holding up his widow. I heard about the abduction a week ago, and she was in here yesterday pleadin' with me to do something. It's a conspiracy, Custis. Sally ain't the only one in town who's had this happen to her."

"How much ransom are the bastards asking for?"

"Twenty thousand."

"That's a lot of money. Can that bundle Tom left her cover it?"

"He left her better'n sixty thousand."

"Guess he *was* tightfisted, at that."

"Fortunately, Longarm, this grisly business shouldn't take too long."

"Whenever you say that, chief, I wince."

"I mean it this time, Custis. Sally says there's a gent—name of Sam Deaver—who's got a line on the gents who're behind this here kidnapping. And he's willing to spill what he knows for a consideration."

"How much of a consideration?"

"Five hundred."

"That's some consideration."

"Sally's willing to pay him, Longarm. But I don't have to tell you that it would not make me a bit unhappy if we could crack this without her having to fork over a red cent—to Deaver or anyone else."

"How do I find this fellow?"

"Sally told me he's waiting for you right now in room 410 at the Colorado Hotel in Golden."

"What's his connection to her?"

"Deaver used to be her gardener."

"Where will I find the widow?"

"She lives in a big brownstone on Lookout Hill, off Dulcimer Street, as I remember. You won't have no trouble finding it. It's a showplace with lots of windows and turrets. But I don't want Sally disturbed if you don't have to. She's pretty damned upset by this business."

Longarm got to his feet. "There's just one thing, Billy."

"What's that?"

"Shouldn't the local authorities be handling this?"

"The local authorities be damned!" Vail said emphatically. "I want *you* on this! Besides, Tom was a veteran. Like I said, he served with Zach Taylor. It ain't constitutional to steal the body of a U.S. Army veteran, one that's been buried with full military honors, including an honor guard from Camp Weld! I already checked with Washington, Custis. Since four o'clock yesterday—when I got a confirmation from the War Department—this here's federal business!"

Longarm grinned at Vail. "Calm down, Billy. I just asked."

Billy Vail took out his handkerchief and mopped his brow, then got up and escorted Longarm to the door. "Just so you know how I feel about it, Custis," he said, resting his hand on Longarm's shoulder. "Leave as soon as you can. You can hire a mount at the Diamond K and be in Golden in less than an hour."

"I'll be there by this afternoon, chief."

"Good."

Vail opened the door for Longarm and stepped back to let him through. "Just get them ghoulish bastards, Custis."

Longarm arrived in Golden later than he had expected, a little after six in the evening. He left the roan he had rented from the Diamond K at the town livery across from the Colorado Hotel, then crossed the street and kept on past the hotel to the alley alongside it. He paused at the head of the alley and lit a cheroot. He took a few puffs on it while he looked around, then ducked down the alley.

He cut behind the hotel and passed two privies before he came to the hotel's rear entrance. He mounted the low porch and pushed open the door and found himself in a narrow hallway. He moved down it until he came to the backstairs. Mounting them swiftly and silently, he came to the fourth-floor landing. Two strides brought him to room 410. He knocked lightly on the door. There was no response. He knocked again, louder, and was about to turn away when he noticed the door sagging inward slightly under the force of his knock. He pushed the door open all the way and stepped into the room.

Sam Deaver was waiting for him in a chair by the window. He was facing Longarm, his back to the light, his battered engineer's cap tipped to one side, the handle of a bowie knife protruding from the front of his bib overalls. On the floor under his chair a dark puddle of blood had not yet dried. Longarm kicked the door shut behind him and approached the dead man. Deaver's sagging cheeks were covered with a gray fuzz; his eyes were wide and staring, looking up in startled surprise at Longarm, his toothless mouth sagging open. A friend—or someone he knew pretty damn well—had walked calmly up to him and planted the bowie in his chest before the poor son of a bitch knew what was happening to him.

Longarm went through the man's pockets and found nothing unusual, only a box of wooden matches from the Last Chance Saloon. As he pocketed the matches, the hinges on the closet door beside him squeaked. He started to turn. Something heavy and unyielding struck the side of his head, knocking off his hat. He staggered back under the force of the blow; the back of his knees struck the edge of a chair, and he tumbled awkwardly to the floor.

His attacker—a gaunt, grizzled man in his forties—tried to club him a second time with a huge Walker Colt. On one knee, Longarm reached up and grabbed the man's wrist and flung him angrily to one side. The fellow seemed as insubstantial as a dried reed and went spinning across the room, his back slamming into the wall, his head crunching into the plaster. Before Longarm could get back up onto his feet, his attacker flung open the door and vanished out the doorway. Longarm heaved himself upright and plunged out of the room after him. But the blow to his head had not been without consequence, and before he could take more than a few steps down the hallway, dizziness overcame him. The walls and ceiling seemed to exchange place. He reached out and hung on to the wall, waiting for the vertigo to pass. As soon as he could manage it he continued down the now empty hallway. At the head of the stairs, he paused to listen. He heard nothing, not a single retreating footfall.

Fingering gingerly at the rapidly growing lump on the side of his head, he walked on wobbly feet back to Sam Deaver's room and picked up his hat, then eased himself wearily down onto the edge of the bed, keeping a speculative eye on his silent companion.

After a few moments he judged himself fit enough to negotiate the flight of stairs and ducked out of the room, pulled the door shut behind him, and left the hotel the same way he had entered it.

The three-story brownstone that topped Lookout Hill was, as Billy Vail had mentioned, a mess of bay windows, corner turrets, and roofs, gingerbread trim lining nearly every eave. It had been a weary trudge up the hill, and pausing now to gaze up at the gloomy structure, Longarm figured there had to be at least twenty rooms in the place, each one as drafty as the next, and maybe some bats in the belfry. Silhouetted against the bloodred evening sky, the brownstone looked to be the perfect place for a grieving widow to huddle in black while she waited for the return of her husband's embalmed remains.

Longarm walked up the long red sandstone walk set between the rows of chestnut trees. He mounted the steps to the broad veranda, crossed it, and knocked on the impressive, paneled door. After a moment he heard a dim rustle of silk behind it, then the sound of a chain dropping from its guard; the knob turned and the door was pulled back. A frail little lady not much taller than five feet, her white hair in a tight bun stared up at him with the fierce look of a bird of prey, a double-barreled Greener held firmly in her bony hands.

"And who in blazes be you, mister?"

Longarm took off his hat. "Name's Long, ma'am. U.S. deputy marshal. Billy Vail sent me. Are you Long Tom's widow?"

Her face softened somewhat. "I am that. You say Billy sent you?"

"That's right."

"Step in, step in. It's gettin' chilly out. No sense coolin' off the whole house."

Longarm stepped into the entrance hall and dropped his hat onto a coat tree standing in the corner. The widow leaned the shotgun against the wall and shut the door firmly, replaced the chain, then swept ahead of him into the sitting room. Longarm followed in after her, grateful for the low fire glowing in the huge fireplace.

The widow's skirt was black, but her silk blouse was white, its snug collar held in place with a turquoise brooch, her long sleeves ending in ruffles at her wrists. On her feet bright red slippers flashed. As she sat down in a high-backed upholstered chair, a footrest in front of it, she flung a green knitted shawl over her bony shoulders. With a quick nod of her birdlike head she indicated the sofa.

"Sit down, deputy," she told him.

Longarm did as he was bid. The room—paneled in heavy mahogany, each panel set off with a gilt lining—was twice the size of the average sitting room. A thick Oriental rug sat on the floor. The fireplace filled the far wall, a coal scuttle sitting alongside it, next to the poker and andirons. Two large Tiffany lamps glowing on dark mahogany end tables sent their soft, luxuriant light over the walls and furniture. A full-length portrait of the late Tom Sanders frowned imperiously down at them. The late tycoon was standing with one thumb tucked into his yellow vest, his stomach thrust out proudly, its ample expanse crossed by a gleaming gold watch chain.

"Did you see Sam yet?" the widow asked. "Did he tell you where to find the bastards what stole Tom's body?"

"Sam Deaver's dead, Mrs. Sanders."

"Dead?"

"Murdered, to be more precise."

The little woman pulled her head back, then frowned at Longarm, her face a bedsheet white. For a moment her face resembled that of a bleached skull.

"Murdered? Is that what you said, deputy?"

"Sorry I put it that bluntly, ma'am," Longarm said. "But that's the plain, unvarnished truth of it. When I entered Sam's hotel room, I found him dead in his chair."

She cleared her throat. "That's . . . most distressing," she managed. "Do you know who killed him?"

"I have no idea. The murderer was close enough to give me some trouble," Longarm admitted, pointing to the lump on his head. "But he got clean away. I'm hoping you can give me a lead on him."

"You saw him then?"

"I saw a man with wild eyes, Mrs. Sanders. And a gaunt, unshaven face. He tried to club me with a Walker Colt."

"Dick Pratt," she whispered. "That'd be Dick Pratt."

"You got any idea where I might be able to find him?"

"The Last Chance Saloon, deputy. But I don't

understand it. Dick was Sam's friend."

"It makes sense to me. It looked to me like Sam knew the person who killed him."

"How was he killed?"

"A knife in the chest."

"How . . . horrible. Poor Sam."

She got to her feet and started from the room, appearing to sway for a moment. Longarm got up quickly, intending to reach out and assist her.

"Stay where you are, deputy," she said, waving him off. "I'm . . . just going into the kitchen to . . . fix some tea."

Longarm sat down again, realizing that what she wanted was a chance to get off by herself for a moment to pull herself together. She vanished from the room, and he heard her quick steps as she moved down the hallway to the kitchen.

When she returned about ten minutes later, she was carrying a silver serving tray containing a teapot and two cups and saucers, sugar, and cream. She put the tray down on a teakwood table beside the sofa. Her eyes were slightly red-rimmed, but her color had returned and she appeared to have regained her composure.

"Cream and sugar?" she asked, pouring Longarm's tea.

"Just sugar."

With a little gleaming silver spoon she spooned two sugars into his tea, stirred thoroughly, then handed him the cup and saucer. For herself she was a bit more generous with the cream and sugar.

"Sam was with Tom and me for close on to fifteen years," she explained with a soft sigh, "before we had to let him go."

"You fired him?"

"Yes."

"Why?"

"He drank too much and he gambled away whatever we gave him. Tom and I were both sorry to dismiss him. He had a green thumb if anyone had. His roses missed him very much, and so did we, despite his profligate ways."

"Who were his friends in town?"

"Birdie Lombard as his drinking and gambling buddy—along with Dick Pratt. Tom and I warned him not to hang around with that crowd. But of course he never listened. He was a very stubborn man."

"I understand he wanted a reward for his help in locating your husband's body."

"I did not begrudge him the money, deputy. As usual, I suspect, he was deeply in debt."

"To whom?"

"Walt Kennedy, more than likely. A gent from New York. He's been here only three years, but he's moved in fast. Right now he's the owner of the Last Chance and has managed to get his hooks into a great many other establishments as well. He's an accomplished gambler, deputy. He cheats, of course. Everyone knows that. But no one has ever caught him at it. I think that's the attraction—why so many try to beat him."

"I found a matchbox in Pratt's pocket, said Last Chance Saloon on it."

She nodded. "That's no surprise to me. That's where he lived almost." She sighed. "Well, if he owed Kennedy anything, Kennedy will have to wait for it—for a long, long time."

"Had Sam mentioned who he suspected might have taken your husband's remains?"

"No. I ran into Sam in town while I was shopping. He spoke to me for only a moment and seemed very nervous. All he had time to tell me was that he felt sure he was onto something. I told him I was going in to Denver to see Marshal Vail. He told me how much he wanted and that he'd be waiting in his hotel room today for whoever Billy sent."

"You say he acted jumpy. You mean he thought someone was watching him?"

"How would I know what Sam was thinking, deputy? At any rate, he vanished down the street before I could question him any further."

"What can you tell me about the local law?"

"You mean Jim Boyd, the town marshal?"

"Yes."

"Boyd drinks too much and gambles too much. I wouldn't put it past him to be in league with them what took my Tom. He's into every other dirty little racket in town. And his two deputies take their cue from their master."

"I see. Too bad. I was hoping the marshal would help me to collar Dick Pratt. With a noose hanging over his head, he might have a lot to tell us about this gang of grave robbers."

"Well, you won't get much help from the marshal," she snapped bitterly. "If I were you, I wouldn't trust him as far as I could throw a piano."

Frowning, Longarm nodded, willing to accept her appraisal of the local lawman and his deputies.

The widow finished her tea and leaned back, her sharp, birdlike eyes regarding Longarm closely. "So what now, deputy? Dick Pratt has already left his mark on you, and you ain't been in town long enough to cool your heels. Marshal Vail said he was sending the best he had. Are you the best?"

"Billy likes to exaggerate."

"Mebbe so. But I trust this time he wasn't." She looked him over speculatively. "You certainly look big enough."

Longarm put down his own cup and saucer. "Do you have the ransom note?"

"It's in the desk," she said.

She got up and moved briskly into the next room. Longarm got up and followed after her. She lit a lamp, then opened the desk and took a folded slip of paper from one of the cubbyholes and handed it to Longarm. He unfolded the letter and found himself puzzling over a barely decipherable scrawl. It was in pencil, and read:

Widow Sanders,

We got your husband's remains. Give us twenty thousand if you want to see his body again.

Leave the bank notes with Silas MacGregor by Saturday morning. We warn you. Don't go to the law. If the law comes down on us, you will never see your loved one's remains again.

Don't mess with us. We mean bisness. We are desprit men. So do like we say.

Longarm looked up. "You planning to pay this ransom, Mrs. Sanders?"

Her ribbed lips became a sharp line. "Not one penny, deputy. Tom would roll over in his grave if I gave in to these vultures. But I do want him back!"

"Could I keep this note?"

"I have no further use for it."

Longarm refolded it and dropped it into his side pocket. "Who's this Silas MacGregor?"

"He's the undertaker. Runs the Heavenly Rest Funeral Parlor." A faint smile brightened her wrinkled features. "Only Silas don't like it if you call him an undertaker. He prefers mortician. Or better yet, funeral director."

"Did he make any effort to explain how the kidnappers could've gotten into his vaults?"

"He did not. I contacted him as soon as I received the ransom note and checked Tom's coffin, the best money could by. It was empty."

"So MacGregor is the middleman."

"The middleman?"

"The one holding the ransom."

"He would be—if I gave in to these vultures."

"You've spoken to MacGregor about this?"

"I have. When I told him in no uncertain terms that I had no intention of paying these ghouls one red cent." She sighed and shook her gray head. "Of course, Silas is most distressed by this business. He feels terrible, being put in the middle like this. Still,

I can understand his dilemma. He has no choice. The kidnappers warned him that they would burn him out if he did not cooperate—and they've also warned him that no one will see the remains of their loved ones until everyone has paid up and the kidnappers are free to leave."

"Then if you don't pay, they will carry out that threat."

"It's just a threat, deputy. You must know that. How can anyone put credence in the words of these monsters. I pay it no heed."

Longarm nodded.

"Thank you, Mrs. Sanders. That'll do for now."

"You going to get my Tom back for me, young man?"

"If not, I'll get the bastards who took him."

She nodded decisively. "That's what Tom would've said. Good luck to you, young man."

She wrapped her shawl more snugly about her narrow shoulders and accompanied him to the door. She reached into the corner for her shotgun before opening it for him. Mildly amused at her action, Longarm put his hat on and stepped out onto the porch.

It was nearly pitch-dark by this time. As he turned to the widow to bid her good night a gunshot rang out from behind one of the trees lining the walk. A piece of the doorjamb inches from Longarm's head leaped into the air. In that same instant the widow Sanders stepped boldly out onto the porch in front of Longarm, flung up her shotgun, and let fly one of the barrels at a shadowy figure fleeing across the lawn and down the hill. She tracked him calmly and loosed the second barrel. The running figure appeared to stagger momentarily, but managed to keep on, and in a moment he had vanished from sight below the crest of the hill.

The widow lowered her shotgun.

"Watch yourself, deputy," she advised him. "Looks like you ain't welcome in Golden."

Stepping back inside, she shut the door firmly behind her.

Chapter 2

When Longarm reached the hotel, there was a milling, curious crowd growing in the street in front of it. He nudged his way through it and entered the lobby. The desk clerk greeted him nervously, his eyes flicking toward the stairs as he did so.

"A room for the night," Longarm said.

"Yes, sir," said the clerk absently. He swung the register around and handed Longarm a pen.

Longarm signed the register and handed the pen back to the clerk. "What's all the fuss?" he asked.

"There's been a . . . murder."

"A murder?"

"Yes. They're bringing the body down now."

"I hope you're not giving me the same room."

The clerk glanced quickly down at Longarm's signature. "Certainly not, Mr. Long. Your room is on the second floor. Two-oh-three."

"Good."

Longarm held out his hand for the key.

The clerk gave it to him and Longarm headed for the stairs. Halfway up he had to pause and tuck himself to one side as Sam Deaver's body, wrapped in an army blanket, was carried past him by four townsmen. The town marshal and his two deputies followed behind them. As they passed him Longarm reached out and took the marshal's arm.

"Marshal Boyd, could I have a word with you?"

Frowning irritably, Boyd halted. His deputies moved on past him down the stairs.

"What do you want, mister?"

"Long's the name, Custis Long."

"The famous Longarm, huh? I heard about you."

Longarm had no comment. He waited.

"I can't talk to you now. I got a dead man on my hands," Boyd said. "See me later in my office down the street."

"Thank you, Marshal. I'll be there."

With a curt nod, the man turned away from Longarm and hurried on down the stairs.

An hour later, Longarm strode into the town marshal's office and found Boyd alone, tacking up a wanted poster on the wall beside the jail-cell door. He turned on Longarm's entrance and greeted him with a nod.

He was a thickset bull of a man with the raw, coarse complexion of a heavy drinker, and at the moment he had the unhappy, shifting eyes of someone who badly needed a shot of rotgut. His star was pinned to a grease-stained vest that was missing a few buttons. His tan Stetson badly needed blocking and cleaning.

Longarm slumped into a wooden chair beside the town marshal's wooden, flat-topped desk. Boyd sat in his armchair behind the desk, pulled out a drawer, and lifted a glass and a silver whiskey flask out of it.

"You want a belt?" he asked Longarm.

"Not right now."

"Suit yourself," the marshal said. He poured a solid two fingers into the glass.

"What I came in to report first off," Longarm said, "is that a little while ago someone took a potshot at me outside the widow Sanders's house."

Downing the whiskey in one quick flip of his head, Boyd set down the glass and cocked an eyebrow at Longarm.

"Missed, did he?"

"That's not the point."

"So what is the point?" the marshal asked, pouring himself another shot.

"Whoever it was, the widow winged him with her shotgun. I think he's hurt bad enough to need medical help."

"That so?"

"I'd like you to keep your eyes and ears open. If you hear of anyone looking for a doctor to patch up a buckshot wound, I'd appreciate it if you'd let me know."

"Sure."

"Who *is* the doc in town?"

"Doc Dante. He's a lush."

"Is that right?" Longarm remarked, watching the marshal downing his second libation.

"Yeah, that's so," Boyd growled, wiping his mouth with the back of his hand.

"Where's his office?"

"You want him you'll find him in the Last Chance, more'n likely."

"One more thing, Marshal."

"What is it?"

"I think I can help you with this murder of Sam Deaver."

"Can you now?"

"I was supposed to meet Deaver in that hotel room. But he was murdered before I got there. He told the widow he had a line on who's been abducting these dead bodies for ransom. He was going to help me track them down."

"That so?"

"Yes, Marshal. That's so."

"Say, listen, Long. No one in town cares a pinch of coon shit who killed Sam Deaver. He was a deadbeat. He owed everybody. If you believe he knew anything about these stolen corpses, that don't mean I have to believe it, too. He'd say anything to get a stake. He was a lush and liar. One more thing, Longarm. This here's my town and my responsibility. I don't need any federal marshals ridin' in here telling me how to do my job."

"That was not my intention, Marshal. But I think

it would be wise of us to join forces."

"Well, maybe that's what you think. It ain't what I think," Boyd replied bluntly. "So you go on about your business, and I'll go on about mine."

"If that's the way you want it, Boyd."

"That's the way I want it."

Boyd put the flask back into his desk and stood up, indicating that the interview was over. Longarm got to his feet also, turned, and strode from the office.

A back room at the Last Chance was crowded with five unhappy men. One disheveled man, rank with the smell of horse piss and manure, was slumped on a bench, doing his best to keep out of the way. In the corner a fellow in a tweed suit with a toothpick sticking out of the corner of his mouth was watching with little emotion, his arms crossed. He looked bored, vaguely contemptuous—like someone from another planet watching the antics of fool natives. Walt Kennedy—immaculate in a white silk shirt and sharply creased dark trousers and red silk vest, tall, slim, his dark hair slicked back—was standing by an army cot, the doctor beside him bent over the bloody figure on the cot. His inspection completed, the doctor stepped back and turned to Kennedy.

"Can I see you outside, Walt?"

Without a word, the gambler turned, squeezed past the fellow on the bench, and left the room, the doctor following out after him.

"Well, doc?" the gambler asked as soon as the door was shut behind them. "How bad is he?"

Dr. Emile Dante cleared his throat and indicated

the bar with a toss of his head. "Well, first off, Walt, I could use a little lubrication about now," he said.

Walt turned quickly, caught the barkeep's eye, and with a quick jab of his finger, pointed at the doc. Then he turned around and led the way over to a table. The doc followed Walt and the two men sat down at a table against the wall that gave them a clear view of the back-room door. When the doc saw the barkeep approaching, he brightened. He was a frail, wasted man with an untidy Vandyke beard, bloodshot eyes, and long, trembling fingers. As soon as the barkeep slapped the bottle and glass down in front of him, he reached out quickly, pulled the shot glass and bottle closer to him, and with trembling hands filled his shot glass to the top and an ace beyond; then, frantic not to lose a drop, he leaned forward and tipped up the glass swiftly, downing the contents in one swift gulp. He wiped his mouth with the back of his hand, his eyes bright, his hands steadier now—already a new man—and poured himself another shot.

Walt placed his palm over the top of the glass. "Dammit, doc. I asked you a question. How bad is Dick's wound?"

"Pretty damn bad," the doc said, his voice trembling slightly as he peered at his lifeblood poised under Walt's palm. "The arm's got to come off. No way can I save it."

"Off, you say?" Walt pulled back his hand and sat back in his chair, frowning at the doc.

"You saw his arm. That widow's buckshot shredded it from his shoulder to his wrist. The elbow's not there anymore. I'm tellin' you. There's no way I can save it."

Walt shook his head. "That crazy old dame."

The doc tossed down his third whiskey. He was coming alive rapidly. "Hell, Walt. Loosen up. Old Long Tom would be proud."

"She had no right to stick her nose in. It was that damned U.S. deputy Dick was after."

The doc looked shrewdly at Walt. "Seems to me you got caught sending a mouse after a lion. No wonder you got a bloody mess in your back room." He sighed wearily. "Well, when do you want me to operate?"

"You cut off the arm?"

"That's the only thing'll save him." The doc frowned in sudden concern. "He'll bleed to death if I don't take off that arm and cauterize the stump."

Walt grinned meanly at him. "Well, not here. Not in my back room."

The doc shrugged. "It don't matter where I do it, just so's it gets done." He sighed. "I could use another bottle, Walt. This one's nearly empty."

Walt got up from his chair. "Tell the barkeep you got my okay to start a fresh tab."

The doc brightened. "Thanks, Walt."

"Just keep your mouth shut."

"It's already buttoned," the doc assured him.

Walt turned and crossed to the back room. Pushing into it, he walked over to the cot and looked down at Dick Pratt, the gambler's cold dark eyes showing nothing. Pratt was moaning slightly, his eyes screwed shut in agony. What was left of his arm rested on his chest, wrapped in an old tablecloth, the blood soaking through it turning the white-checked cloth into a massive red stain. Under the cot, a growing pool of blood gave a pretty clear indication of how much blood Pratt was losing. The doc was probably right. If they didn't get that arm off and fix the stump, Pratt was a dead man.

Pratt opened his eyes and saw Walt looking down at him.

"Jesus, Walt," he groaned. "Where's the doc? Where's he gone? I can't stand the pain!"

"He wants to cut off your arm, Dick."

Dick's eyes bugged out in horror. "No!" he cried. "Don't let him! Tell him he's got to fix it—he's got to sew it up!"

"Yeah, sure. I'll tell him."

"Oh, God. Thanks, Walt," Dick gasped. "Thanks."

Walt turned to the man on the bench. His name was Birdie Lombard. He was the one who had brought Dick into the back room, and Walt blamed him for this whole mess. The idea had been for him to wait for the U.S. deputy in Deaver's room, kill Deaver and the deputy, leaving the bowie in the deputy's hands to implicate him. A simple enough job, but Birdie and Pratt had botched it.

"Birdie, was it you sent this asshole up Lookout Hill to take out the deputy?"

"I swear it was his idea," Birdie said. "I told him he was crazy going after the deputy like that, but he said he wanted to finish it."

Walt turned to look down at Pratt.

"That right, asshole?"

"I almost had him, Walt. He came right into Sam's room like we knew he would. I hit him hard—on the head. He went down, but he reached up and flung me off him like I was no heavier than a fly. I followed him to the widow's and would've had him. How'd I know she was totin's a shotgun?"

"Well, you know now."

"Yeah. Yeah. Walt . . . please, get the doc back in here, will you?" Pratt's face twisted in agony. "I can't bear this pain."

"Well, you'll have to."

"Walt, for Christ's sake!"

"You got to wait until I close the place. Now, shut up."

Walt stepped back from the cot and turned to the other one standing in the corner with his arms crossed. "John, think you can help Birdie get Pratt out of here."

Thomaris glanced with distaste at Pratt. "Ain't the doc comin' back in here to stop all this bleeding?"

"Take him over to Birdie's room and I'll send the doc over there to fix him up."

"Christ, there'll be blood all over."

"You going to help out, or what, John?"

"I sure as hell didn't come this far to lug a dying man around. That ain't my specialty."

Walt grinned at him. "What is your specialty, John?"

"All right, all right. I'll help Birdie."

"Thanks, John," said Birdie.

Walt started for the door. "Just get him the hell out of here."

Walt left the room and slammed the door behind him. The doc was still at his table. He looked over at him and waved. A dead soldier sat in front of him, a new whiskey bottle beside it.

Dante was well on his way.

Walt strode to the rear of the saloon, then turned up a flight of stairs leading to his private apartment on the second floor. He entered it without knocking and walked into his living room, where the town marshal and his two deputies were waiting for him. There was a bottle of Walt's best whiskey in Boyd's hands, an empty glass on the coffee table in front of him.

Walt took the whiskey and the glass off the table and poured himself a drink. "Pratt's hurt bad," he told Boyd and the other two.

"How bad?" Boyd asked.

"The poor stupid son of a bitch is bleedin' to death." He downed his drink. "That crazy widow blew his arm to shreds. And right now the doc's too drunk to operate."

"So what do we do now?"

"We take care of that U.S. deputy before he ruins everything."

"You goin' to send Birdie after him?"

"That asshole?"

"Then who?"

Walt grinned at Boyd. "I'm going to send the law after him."

"The law?"

"That's right, Boyd. You."

When Walt saw the look on Boyd's face, he handed the whiskey bottle and glass back to him.

• • •

Silas MacGregor told Longarm he was too busy to speak to him at the moment and politely ushered him into the Heavenly Rest Funeral Parlor's somber waiting room. The big lawman was not alone for long. Soon after he sat down, a young lady in her late twenties entered. The rustle of her silk skirt filled the room as she crossed in front of him. She glanced at him discreetly, kept going to the far corner and sat down in a high-backed upholstered chair, crossed her legs, and rested her white-gloved hands in her lap.

Her face had clean, classic lines, her cheekbones were high, her eyes two gleaming emerald shards. She was wearing a white straw boater that could barely contain the luxuriant abundance of her gold tresses, and under her pink cotton blouse, her burgeoning breasts swelled provocatively above a wasp-thin waist. There was an air of the East about her, not only in her frank, bold gaze, but in the daring length of her bottle-green skirt, which was short enough to reveal her ankles completely. He sensed that she was not only traveling alone, but was more than likely one of those modern women who were beginning to work in business offices back east, manning one of them newfangled Underwood typewriting machines.

Longarm straightened in his chair and pondered how he might initiate a conversation despite the fact that they had not been formally introduced. He fiddled with his hat and cleared his throat a couple of times and was about to give up when the young lady spoke up clearly.

"Are you new here in Golden?"

"Yes, I am," Longarm told her. "Rode in yesterday."

"My, that sounds so *Western*."

"Well, that's where we are."

She smiled. "My name's Jean Langly. I'm from New York."

"Pleased to meet you, ma'am. I'm from Denver. My name's Custis Long. I'm a U.S. deputy."

Her eyebrows shot up. "Oh, a Western police officer."

"That's right, ma'am." He glanced at the door to Silas MacGregor's office. "Someone you know pass on?"

"No. Fortunately. I am just making a few . . . inquiries."

"Oh."

"About disappearing corpses."

Startled, Longarm said, "Here? In Golden?"

"No. In New York. It was some time ago."

"Then you're . . ."

"A private investigator."

"Looks like we're in the same business."

"Apparently."

"Maybe we ought to combine forces. Two heads are better than one, they say."

She smiled coolly. "Perhaps."

"Where are you staying?"

"The hotel."

The door to Silas MacGregor's office opened and the mortician stepped into the waiting room.

"Sorry to have kept you, deputy," the funeral director said. "I can see you now."

"I can wait," Longarm said. "See Miss Langly first."

"As you wish." MacGregor turned. "Miss Langly?"

She got to her feet and smiled at Longarm. "Thank you, Mr. Long. That's kind of you."

"Not at all," said Longarm.

Miss Langly followed MacGregor into his office. In less than a quarter of an hour the funeral director escorted Miss Langly from his office. On her way out through the waiting room, she met Longarm's eyes and held them for a moment, assuring Longarm that the two of them would find each other again and soon.

Longarm followed MacGregor into his office.

"Been busy, have you?" Longarm commented, making himself comfortable in a chair beside the mortician's desk.

"Yes, very," Silas MacGregor said, rounding his desk and bending his long frame into his wooden armchair. He was a tall, angular gentleman in his late forties with bushy brows, thinning ink-black hair, a long neck, and a prominent Adam's apple.

He cleared his throat nervously. "It seems a local ne'er-do-well got himself murdered last night."

"A feller called Sam Deaver, you mean."

"You knew him?"

"Only in passing."

MacGregor looked a little more closely at Longarm. "That so? Well, now, to the business at hand. I understand Mrs. Sanders has retained you to look into her husband's disappearance—or more accurately, the disappearance of his already embalmed remains."

"He hasn't disappeared, MacGregor. He was kidnapped."

"Yes, of course," MacGregor replied quickly. "That's what I meant."

"Tom's widow told me all about this business. I have the ransom note that was sent to her. I assume she has made it clear that she has no intention whatsoever of paying this ransom."

"So she has informed me."

"Meanwhile, you have been accepting the ransom payments from those widows willing to pay."

"Unfortunately, yes."

"I understand, MacGregor. Mrs. Sanders told me of the threat you are working under."

"It is a threat I do not take lightly."

"This money you receive. Where do you keep it?"

"I keep none of it," he said. "Almost as soon as it is delivered to me I am relieved of it—much to my relief, I can assure you."

"Someone comes for it?"

"Yes."

"Who?"

"A masked man. I have never seen his face. He comes late at night when I am instructed to keep only this single lamp on the desk lit. As a result, I am able to catch only a fleeting glimpse of him. He comes and goes in less than a minute."

Silas MacGregor was too honest a man to prevaricate successfully. Longarm could see in the shift of his eyes and the tone of his voice that this dime-novel tale of a masked man sneaking in at night to take the ransom from him was a lie. MacGregor knew the man who came for the ransom money, but was evidently under strict orders not to reveal his identity.

"At the rate they're going, this gang must have quite a haul by now," Longarm commented.

"Considerable."

"What else can you tell me?"

"Precious little, I am afraid."

"Well, where was the body taken from?"

"Our vaults."

"Vaults?"

"Where we keep the deceaseds' remains before interment," MacGregor explained patiently.

"How long do you usually keep the remains in your vaults."

"Depends on the time of the year. This dried adobe soil resembles concrete. Our best time for interment is in the spring before the ground has had a chance to dry out."

"You mean you keep these bodies that long, waiting for a chance to bury them?"

"We have no choice."

"Why not burn them?"

His bushy eyebrows went up a notch. "My dear sir, the loved ones of the dearly departed would not hear of such a desecration."

"Well, don't they—the bodies, I mean—become powerful rank, after all that time?"

MacGregor chuckled, the lines of his long face softening somewhat. He leaned back in his chair and shook his head. "I can understand why you would think that, Mr. Long. But we at the Heavenly Rest Funeral Home have ways of taking care of that. Science, it seems, has come to our aid. Our embalming process is more than sufficient to prevent the corruption of the flesh—for a considerable time, I might add."

"That so?"

"Do you remember the kidnapping of Lincoln's corpse?"

"I heard of it, yes."

He leaned forward, the hint of a smile on his face. Silas MacGregor was a skilled artisan and evidently enjoyed nothing more than discussing the tricks of his trade. "When Lincoln's stolen coffin was recovered by the Secret Service, they naturally wanted to make sure it was Lincoln's body inside."

"I can understand that."

"So they cut a neat opening in the lead-lined lid and shone a light inside. Though Lincoln's body had been in there quite a spell, they were able to recognize his gaunt features. It was Honest Abe, all right. But thanks to the embalming fluid, his skin had turned as dark as worn saddle leather. Otherwise, he was as good as new."

Longarm shook his head. "That sure as hell must be strong stuff you're using."

MacGregor chuckled. "Does that answer your question?"

"It does. When can I inspect this vault of yours?"

"Well, not now, I am afraid. I'm quite busy. I have to deal with Sam Deaver's untimely demise."

"Some other time then."

"Of course."

Longarm stood up. "Before I go," he said, "I would

appreciate the names of the other funeral homes. I assume they've been experiencing the same untimely withdrawals."

"Yes," MacGregor said glumly, his long face growing longer. "They have indeed. I'll be glad to give you the names, but you must understand our predicament. We have all been warned that if any of us raise any kind of an alarm, none of these widows will ever see their loved one's remains again."

"I'm not about to raise any alarm. I'm as anxious to keep this ugly business a secret as you are—for now. I'm just investigating."

"On behalf of Mrs. Sanders, you mean."

"Yes, on behalf of Mrs. Sanders."

MacGregor sighed. "Well, then, from what I've heard, the remains of two other recently deceased men have been taken from the Golden Funeral Home on Baker Street."

"On Baker Street."

"A side street two blocks down from the hotel."

"Anyplace else?"

"There's only one other funeral home. O'Brian's. And I am afraid he's been having the same . . . difficulties."

Longarm thanked MacGregor and left.

Stepping out onto the dark street a few moments later, he looked around, hoping to catch a glimpse of that young lady from New York. But she was nowhere in sight. She had skedaddled back to the hotel by this time. She sure as hell wouldn't be found in the Last Chance—or any of the other less opulent saloons lining the street.

He took out a cheroot, lit up, and crossed the street to the hotel. Three bodies kidnapped for sure, and from the looks of things, these three were only the tip of the iceberg.

He remembered Vail assuring him that clearing up this business wouldn't take long.

Chapter 3

The next morning, after a fruitless quest for Dr. Emile Dante, Longarm visited Jim Daniel, the owner and director of the Golden Funeral Parlor. The mortician was a fat little bald man in a dark blue suit, stiff high collar, and tie. As he got out from behind his desk to greet Longarm he pushed his gold-rimmed spectacles hastily up onto his nose.

"I am afraid I can only give you a few minutes, deputy," he said, shaking Longarm's hand once. The man's pudgy palm was damp, limp. It was obvious he did not really want to talk to Longarm this morning. "Won't you sit down."

Longarm took off his hat and sat in the chair by

Daniel's desk. "It was good of you to see me," he said.

"Well, I *am* busy," Daniel said, hustling back around his desk and squeezing back into his chair. "I suppose you've come about these terrible kidnappings."

"What can you tell me about this gang?"

"Only that I dare not do anything to anger them."

"How is it that these kidnappers are having such an easy time taking all these caskets?"

"They aren't taking the caskets—just the bodies."

"Isn't that strange?"

The little man shrugged. "I just assumed it was because it was much simpler and easier for them to steal a body than a casket. A casket would require a flatbed wagon, at least. Not so a body."

"Maybe so. But you still haven't answered my question. Why it is so easy for these ghouls to make off with all these bodies—caskets or no caskets?"

Daniel shrugged helplessly. "Our hands are tied. There's nothing we can do. The gang has threatened to burn us to the ground if we try to interfere—or do anything to stop them. If it wasn't for Mrs. Sanders's stubbornness, you wouldn't be here now."

"What about the town marshal—Boyd?"

"You'll find little help from that quarter, deputy. And neither have we."

"Then why not post private guards—with shotguns?"

"You don't understand, deputy. We can't do that. We have to *cooperate* or lose our business, everything."

"As I understand it, the ransom money is given to you."

"Yes. But I don't have it for long."

"How does that happen?"

"One of their gang visits me after hours and takes it from me."

"And you have no idea what he looks like. What he might be wearing. His style of boots. Anything."

"His face is always hidden by a scarf," Daniel explained dryly, "and to be perfectly frank, deputy, when I look into the bore of his revolver, all I want is for this man to take the money and get out."

"You got any more widows just as stubborn as Sally Sanders? I can't believe they'd all be going along with this."

"There is one, at that."

"What's her name?"

"Eileen Turnbill."

"I think I might give her a visit. How do I get to her place?"

"She lives on Willow Street. It's on the other side of town, near the creek. The big house at the end. You can't miss it."

"Thanks," Longarm said, getting to his feet.

"Not at all, deputy," Daniel told him. "Not at all."

He got out from behind his desk and moved ahead of Longarm to pull open the door for him.

"Good-bye, sir."

Longarm stepped out of the office. His last glimpse of Jim Daniel as he closed the door was of the fellow hastily mopping his bald head. He was obviously pleased all to hell to have gotten rid of Longarm so easily.

Outside on the street he paused to get his bearings and light up another cheroot. Daniel was a man totally intimidated. It was only a few widows in this town, it seemed, who had any backbone left.

He hurried off to meet one of them.

He had no difficulty finding the Turnbill residence on Willow Street. A wreath of black silk had been hung on the front door and the blinds on the four windows facing the street had been pulled shut. It was a large, two-story frame house painted white. Nothing fancy, but a solid, durable home.

Longarm mounted the short flight of flagstone steps and pulled on the doorbell. From deep within the house came the soft peal of chimes. Footfalls approached the door. It was pulled open and Longarm found a little old widow of about twenty-five gazing up at him, first in astonishment, then in pure delight—as if she'd opened a package and found just what she wanted.

"Yes," she asked hopefully, "what can I do for you?"

"Are you Mrs. Eileen Turnbill?" Longarm asked, doffing his hat.

"I am."

"Sorry to bother you this early, ma'am. I'm U.S. Deputy Custis Long. I'd like a word with you, if I may."

Her eager astonishment of a moment before gave

way to something akin to panic. "A U.S. deputy marshal?"

"That's right, ma'am."

"And you want a word with me?" Her face had gone pale. "Why, whatever for?"

"It's about your late husband."

"Alfred?"

"If that was his name."

"But . . . he's dead."

"I know. That's why I'm here. It's about his corpse—or his remains. I understand it has been taken for ransom." He smiled. "I'm here to see what I can do."

"Oh, is *that* why?"

"Yes."

She seemed greatly relieved. "Well, then, *do* come in, deputy. You must forgive me. I'm just not myself lately. This has been a such a tryin' time for me."

"That's all right," Longarm said. "I understand."

She stepped back out of the doorway. Longarm stepped into the front hallway and waited as she closed the door. She took his hat and hung it on the hat tree in the corner, then led the way into the sitting room. It was much smaller than Widow Sanders's sitting room, claustrophobic, in fact. Every stick of furniture in it was draped in black, and so tightly drawn were the drapes that not a single gleam of sunshine penetrated the gloom. A sepulchral silence hung in the air.

She stopped in the middle of the room and turned to face him, a small, delicate creature with an alabaster complexion, a pile of dark, chestnut hair, and dark eyes glowing at him from under lush eyebrows. Her mouth was a sultry pout. Small though she was, there was nothing meager about the urgent swell of her breasts.

"Death is so *final,* deputy." She sighed. "So terrible."

"Yes, ma'am."

"It has left me adrift, bereft. Alone here in this huge, empty house."

"Yes, ma'am."

"With only my memories."

"Afraid so."

A tiny lace handkerchief appeared in her hand. She dabbed pitiably at her eyes. "I just don't know how I'm going to manage."

"You'll just have to bear up, Mrs. Turnbill."

"Yes. I suppose so." She looked around at the dark, lightless front room and wrinkled her nose. "Oh, *do* let us get out of here," she implored him. "Join me in my sewing room. It's next to the kitchen and so much more cheerful."

Longarm was all for that. "You just lead the way, ma'am."

Her sewing room was indeed a relief—as bright as the front room was dark. The drapes were all pulled back, the sun was pouring in, and there were fresh-cut spring flowers on a vase near one window. The only discordant note was the large portrait of the widow's late husband, Alfred, hanging just above the fireplace. The portrait captured with remorseless skill the man's squinty, close-set eyes, his raw, lobster-red face framed in muttonchop whiskers, and the arrogant sweep of his protuberant, chain-draped belly.

The widow, her tears rapidly evaporating, indicated the sofa with a wave.

"Do make yourself comfortable, deputy."

She sat down herself in an easy chair covered with a bright, patchwork quilt. On a stand beside her was a decanter of brandy, a single tall glass beside it.

"Would you care for a drink, deputy?"

"No, ma'am. It's a little early in the day for me. And I have a lot of people to see yet."

"Then you won't mind if I have something. I need it—to keep my nerves under control. I'm sure you understand."

"No need to apologize, ma'am."

She filled the glass about half-full and sipped it, neat. Longarm had the feeling she would have downed the glass in a single gulp had he not been there to observe her.

"First of all, Mrs. Turnbill, as I think you know, you're not the first widow in town who has had her husband's remains taken for ransom."

"Yes, so I heard."

"Sally Sanders's husband's corpse was also kidnapped. Perhaps you know her? She's the one who called me in to see what I could do."

"Yes, I know Sally. Well, now. What can I do to help?"

"Well, first of all, have you received a ransom note?"

"I have."

"Could I see it?"

She reached into her bosom and drew forth a note. Longarm opened it and read substantially the same instructions that had been given to Tom Sanders's widow, except for the amount—which was for one thousand dollars—and the place where the ransom was to be delivered. In this case the middleman was her own undertaker, Jim Daniel.

Longarm handed the note back to her.

"I understand you do not plan to pay the ransom, Mrs. Turnbill."

"I certainly do not."

"Have you been threatened as a result?"

"I have."

"By whom?"

She dug a second time into her bosom and pulled out another note. She handed it to him. He opened it and read:

> Widow Turnbill,
>
> If you dont pay us we will burn your dead husband's body. You will never see it again. You have until next Sunday. After that, we may come visit you ourselves to get the money.
>
> We are warning you. Do not anger us. We are desprit men.

Longarm looked up from the note. "And despite this note, you still aren't going to pay?"

"I am not."

She glanced up nervously at her husband's portrait, as if what she had just said might bring him down off the wall to wreak vengeance.

"You're not afraid they'll come after you?"

"Let them come. I've got a loaded shotgun and I won't hesitate to use it."

"Doesn't it make any difference to you that your husband's body may never be returned?"

She softened under his unrelenting gaze. "But why should it? He's dead, isn't he? I've already paid the funeral expenses. What does it matter if he's buried here in Golden or . . . out in the plains somewhere? He'll be just as dead, no matter where he's planted."

"You don't want a tombstone—a maker of some kind? A place where you can go to lay flowers and look over his grave and . . . meditate on your years together. For some people that's a mighty fine comfort."

"Not for me."

"I see." He glanced up at the portrait.

"What I mean," she added, her voice softening, "is that I hate funerals and cemeteries. Ever since I was a little girl I have been scared to death even to walk past one . . . Oh, why do we have to go on like this?" She dabbed at her eyes. "It's all so cruel. And pointless!"

She bowed her head in her hands. She appeared to be weeping, but Longarm knew better than that.

"Now, now," Longarm said. "No sense in getting all worked up again. I can understand how you'd hate funerals and graveyards. I'm not very partial to them myself."

She looked back up at him and took a deep breath, as if she had just won an important point—and they could now begin to discuss more interesting topics. Her gaze took him in boldly, and he could feel the suppressed hunger in her as she measured his masculinity.

"Are you absolutely sure you won't have a drink, deputy?"

"Well . . . I might take just a snifter, maybe—with water."

"Of course."

She was up instantly and disappeared into the kitchen. He heard her opening cabinets and the clink of glasses, then the squeak of the kitchen pump. She returned with a beaker and a jug of water and set it down on a table beside him, then handed him the brandy. He poured himself as little brandy as possible and filled the glass almost to the brim with water. It was a miserable way to treat good brandy, but if he was going to outsmart this little lady, he was going to have to keep his wits about him.

"Oh, my," Eileen said, "what must you think of me—to let this happen."

They were upstairs in the master bedroom, making full use of its most important single article of furniture. She scooted up so her back rested against the headboard, carefully managing to keep one of her pert breasts uncovered. Its dark nipple was still perkily rigid while the soft glow in her cheeks was a lovely reminder of the torrid fires that had nearly consumed her a few moments before.

"To let *what* happen?" Longarm responded, grinning at her.

"Well, I mean . . ." She wrinkled her nose. "You know . . . what we've just done."

"You mean it was that bad?"

"Oh, no! Mercy me, no." Reaching over, she rested her palm on the wiry carpet of hair covering his chest and began to stroke it gently. "Why, you were simply marvelous."

"You were no slouch yourself."

"Did I . . . surprise you?"

"You did and you didn't."

"Now, Custis, whatever do you mean by that?"

"I figured maybe your last roll in the hay had happened some time ago and you needed this chance to wring yourself out. So I wasn't surprised when you came at me the way you did. I enjoyed it. And I sure was gratified at the wallop a little package like you could deliver."

She tittered, pleased. "Oh, my! You put it so . . . nicely. Wring myself out . . . little package."

"No offense intended. That's just my way of putting it."

"Why, I don't mind at all, not one little bit."

She snuggled closer and dropped her hand to his crotch. "And I haven't finished yet, you can bet. This little package is just warming up."

There was a clock ticking on the bedstand. Longarm glanced at it and saw that it was already ten o'clock.

"Sorry, Eileen, but I can't stay," he told her. "I've been here too long already."

"Now, just stay up here a little while longer,"

she said, her lips caressing his belly, then moving further down.

He felt his groin stirring back to life and tried to ease away from her.

"I really got to get going," he told her feebly.

She laughed softly and insinuated herself up onto his body, her breasts brushing across his chest and setting him afire. Her arms encircled his neck.

"You were right," she whispered huskily. "It *has* been a long time for me. I need you, Longarm."

She kissed him full on the lips, then thrust her tongue through them, the scent of her arousal coming clearly to him as her lips pulsed and sucked eagerly on his. His hand caressed her, then pressed her still closer to him. When she was fully upon him, she reached back and guided him into her, then eased back upon him and began to move with a deep, languorous sensuality.

There was no way he was going to be able to stop now.

It had been a long time for him also.

An hour later she sat in a rocker beside the bed, watching him dress, her robe deliberately untied, allowing it to fall open, giving him a full, provocative view of her gleaming triangle and the still-eager thrust of both nipples. She wanted him to know what he was leaving behind.

As light as a feather, Longarm yanked on his boots and grinned over at her so she'd realize he was now immune to her blandishments. "How about a cup of coffee and something to eat? I missed breakfast."

"Oh, of course," she said, "if *that*'s all you want." She got to her feet, stood for a moment facing him, her eyes smoldering; then with an impish shrug she stuck out her tongue at him and tied her robe more snugly about her.

"Show's over," she said.

She swept out of the bedroom, and a few minutes later, fully dressed, Longarm strode into the dining room and found the table neatly set, a pot of coffee sitting before his place setting. From the kitchen came the sound and mouth-watering odor of ham and eggs frying.

He sat down to wait. When she came in with the platter piled high with freshly cooked ham slices and fried eggs, sunny-side up, and thick slabs of bread, fresh-churned butter, and a pot of mustard, he dove in with an abandon that surprised him. All that good time in bed had made him ravenous.

Watching him, Eileen grinned, delighted. "My goodness, I surely forget how hungry men become . . . afterward."

He poured his second cup of coffee and grinned at her. "You set a fine table, Eileen."

Pleased at the comment, she sat down opposite him and pushed her empty coffee cup at him. He filled it for her, then proceeded to spear a second helping of ham slices.

Watching him, Eileen sighed. "I do so love to watch a hungry man eat."

Longarm laughed and reached for the pot of mustard. "You can believe it, Eileen. I'm hungry."

"This was surely a nice time we had together, Longarm."

"It was pleasant for me also, Eileen."

There was nothing on her plate. She wasn't hungry, it seemed. "I hope you're not wondering, I mean about how I could be so callous, my husband not yet in his final resting place, and all."

"The thought never crossed my mind," he lied.

"Longarm, I have to tell you. I have to tell *someone* or I'll burst."

He looked up from his plate. "Tell me what?"

"How awful it was."

"You mean your husband's death?"

"No," she said with surprising vehemence. "I mean what it was like living with him. He was a cad, Custis. And a miserable, tightfisted boor. Even worse than that, Custis, he was a terrible prude."

"That so?"

"He would only let me make love to him one way. Missionary. Me on the bottom, him on top. Period. He . . . had no imagination, Custis. Not like you. And his body!" She wrinkled her nose in disgust. "It was so soft and flabby. And do you know what, Custis, I honestly think he didn't like to make love to me. Once he even told me I should get hold of myself—that I was too . . . wanton."

"He told you that?"

"Yes," she snapped. "On our wedding night!"

"Poor man. He sure must've missed a lot in life."

"I tried to help him, Custis. I really did. At first

I pitied him. But he was hopeless . . . as cold as a dead fish."

"But now he's dead and you're free of him."

"Yes!"

"How did he die?"

"He . . . just got sick—said he felt poorly and went to bed. I tended him the best I could. But before I knew it, he was carried off. The doc said it was his heart. Just gave out, he said."

"How old was he?"

"Forty-six."

"That's pretty young for a bad ticker."

"Yes . . . I suppose so."

"How long were you two married?"

"Three miserable years."

"Now you're free again. Free of him. Only now you got to pretend that you're in mourning—and you got to keep the house dark in front so all the neighbors will think you're filled with grief—and when you go out, all you can wear is black."

"Yes," she said bitterly. "Yes. That's *just* how it is."

Longarm filled his cup with fresh coffee. "Well, just hang in there a little bit longer, Eileen. A pretty little thing like you won't have to wait long before a gentleman friend will come calling. More than one, I'd say. Then you can put away those widow's weeds."

"I know, Custis. You're right." Then she moved impatiently. "But its only only been three weeks and already I'm ready to fly apart."

For a moment it looked as if she might actually

come unglued and go shooting all over the room. Chuckling, he reached over and closed his big hand over hers.

"Simmer down, Eileen. Simmer down."

She nodded briskly, pulled her hand free, and took a sip of her coffee. "At least you won't find me paying out what Alfred left me just to have his corpse brought back. Not that they would bring him back if I did pay. I know that much."

In the act of reaching for his coffee, Longarm paused and looked across at Eileen. "What do you mean? Paying the ransom wouldn't bring him back?"

"Don't you know?"

"Know what?"

"We've all been warned that if anyone raises the alarm, or goes to the police, the bodies will not be returned. They'll be cremated. Well, I ain't been quiet. I've told everyone. I don't care how many threats I get."

"You mean you've been threatened for talking out?"

"Not from the kidnappers, but from a woman whose husband's body was taken. The note was left in my mailbox. It said for me to keep quiet, that I was making it difficult for everyone—and that if I didn't keep quiet, I would be sorry."

"Who sent it?"

"Juliet Childress."

"Do you have her address?"

She gave it to him.

"Have there been any other recent deaths lately, I mean within the past few days?"

"Yes. Annie Devlin's husband died only two days ago."

"Have the services been held yet?"

"I'm not sure. But the paper would have it."

She left the table and entered the living room, to return a moment later with a copy of the local *Golden Chronicle,* turned to the obituary page, in her hand. Sitting back down at the table, she ran her finger down it, then paused to scan an obituary notice.

"Here it is," she said, glancing up at him. "The church services were held in the First Methodist Church two days ago."

He asked to see the notice. She pushed the paper across the table to him. He found the item. The name of the funeral home and its address was listed as well. He tore the notice out of the paper, folded it neatly, and pocketed it.

"Maybe this is one body I can catch before it gets snatched," he said.

"Longarm, are you going to see Juliet Childress?"

"Yes."

"But why? She's a hateful woman. And she can't tell you any more than I can."

"You haven't told me much."

"What more do you want?"

"I want to know who's behind this—and where in the hell they are keeping all these bodies."

"But I have no idea."

"I'm not saying you do. But tell me, Eileen—if you did know where your husband's body has been taken, would you tell me?"

"I certainly would not."

"In other words, you like things just the way they are."

"Yes."

He had toyed with the idea before, not wanting to believe it. But when he heard her emphatic reply, he knew in that instant what she had done.

"Eileen," he said softly, "did you . . . help Alfred along?"

Her face went white. "Why . . . whatever do you mean?"

"I'm asking if maybe you didn't help your husband on his way."

"But how could you suggest such a thing?"

"You wanted him dead, didn't you?"

"Custis!"

"I was just asking."

"I'm shocked, Custis. That you could think—"

Longarm got to his feet.

"I just wondered is all."

She remained rooted in her seat at the table, her drawn face turned up to his, her eyes wide. He could almost hear the terrified thoughts racing through her mind. *How could he know? What had she said? Would he tell anyone?*

"Don't worry, Eileen," he told her gently. "I won't tell anyone. Just keep your head down and your eyes and ears open. If you find out anything that might help me, I'd appreciate hearing from you. I'll be at the hotel."

He left her still at the table and a moment later stepped out into the bright, fresh air, relieved to hear the door close solidly behind him. Then he yanked his hat down securely and strode off to seek out Juliet Childress, the woman Eileen Turnbill called hateful.

"I understand you wrote Eileen Turnbill a note, warning her to keep quiet. That if she drew attention to what's been going on here, she would ruin everything."

"I did," the widow Childress said without hesitation. "She refuses to pay the ransom for her own dead husband's remains and she will not shut up. None of us who has lost a loved one wants to see her goad these monsters into fleeing without returning the remains."

They were in the widow's front sitting room. There was little sign of her recent mourning period. Her black satin drapes had been drawn back fully, light flooded the room, which was elegantly decorated with upholstered furniture. Potted plants crowded the windows, and the floor was covered with a thick Persian rug. As soon as Longarm had told her who he was and why he was in Golden, the widow had insisted on providing tea and sweetbreads. Longarm sat on a well-upholstered chair holding a cup of tea in one hand and a sweetbread in the other. He was beginning to wish that his tiny porcelain cup contained something a lot stronger than tea.

The widow was in her early fifties, her hair already a glowing white, not a single wrinkle on her her round pink face. She wore no lipstick or rouge, and as she sat back on her sofa she stroked a large white cat, which had leaped onto her lap the moment she sat down.

"Can you give me some idea of the extent of this ugly business?"

"From what I've heard," she said grimly, "the three funeral parlors in town have been steadily plundered."

"Do you know how many bodies have been taken?"

"More than a dozen, I can assure you."

"Have you paid the ransom demanded of you?"

"I have."

"Apart from the widow Sanders and Eileen Turnbill, have any others failed to pay?"

"I have no idea, deputy. The only one I know of personally is Eileen Turnbill. And I can certainly understand why she would not want her husband's body back."

"And why is that?"

She responded icily. "She has probably found out that arsenic poisoning becomes easier to detect the longer a body rests in its grave."

"That's a pretty serious charge."

"Flypaper soup is serious business, deputy. I knew her husband. Alfred wasn't a very nice man, but he was as strong as a horse. There was nothing wrong with his heart. He didn't deserve to go that way, just to make that gold-digging hussy rich. You know where he found her, I presume."

Longarm shifted uneasily under her shrewd gaze. "I can imagine."

"A New Orleans parlor house."

Longarm felt his face darken.

Noting his reaction, the widow uttered a low,

pleasant chuckle. "Now, don't go feeling bad, deputy. You're young and healthy and so is Eileen Turnbill. There's no crime in that." She sighed. "At any rate, she has not paid the ransom that would bring Alfred's body back. But most people have, I'm sure. They're waiting as I am for the bodies of their loved ones to be returned to them."

Longarm shook his head. "In that case, the men behind this must already have reaped a fortune."

"Yes," Juliet Childress said bitterly.

"Tell me, do you have any idea where these bodies could be hidden?"

"Not in Golden, certainly."

"Of course not. I just thought you might have heard something—rumors, maybe."

"Since this happened I've kept pretty much to myself, deputy. You can understand why, I am sure."

"Then you have no idea who might be behind this business?"

"Maybe it's the undertakers," she said. "They certainly haven't been doing a very good job of keeping those dead bodies where they belong. And they're the ones collecting the ransom, don't forget."

"I know. The thought has certainly crossed my mind."

"It's hard to believe, though. MacGregor and Daniel have been here in Golden for years. And the other one as well."

"Have any strangers come to town within the past three or four months?"

She thought a moment, stroking the cat's back.

"Well, now that I think of it, a stranger from back east moved into the Cattleman's Rest about four months ago. He's been very generous with his money. The talk is he's thinking of reopening the Lodestone Mine out near Lookout Mountain."

"Is he onto something, do you think?"

"My Pete spent the best years of his life in those digs. If anyone knew what was left, he did. And when he hung it up, deputy, that was good enough for me. The only thing left on that side of the mountain is rocks and dirt. And piles of slag."

"So that gent must be coming up empty."

"I haven't heard of any new gold rush, have you?"

"No—except for the ransom that's being raked in. How much did you pay?"

"Over three thousand dollars, deputy. And some have paid more—much more."

"This newcomer. Do you have his name?"

"John Thomaris."

"And you say he's staying at the Cattleman's Rest?"

"Yes."

Longarm carefully put down his empty teacup and got to his feet. "Well, thank you, Mrs. Childress," he said. "I believe I've taken enough of your time."

"Not at all," the widow said, getting up and escorting Longarm to the door. "I just hope you won't do anything to rock the boat so I can get my Pete back. His final resting place is waiting for him in the Golden Cemetery, where I hope someday to rest beside him."

"I'll do what I can," Longarm said.

He bid her good-bye and left. It was noon, which meant he might be lucky enough to find Dr. Dante in the Last Chance Saloon. And even if the doctor wasn't there, it would give Longarm the opportunity to lubricate his tonsils with something a whole hell of lot stronger than all this goddamn tea he had been drinking.

Chapter 4

The Last Chance Saloon impressed Longarm. This early in the day, it was almost empty, giving him a good chance to look the place over. It was large, with a ceiling high enough to keep the smoke out of everyone's eyes and ample room for the now empty poker and gaming tables in the rear. The well-stocked mahogany bar ran almost the full length of the establishment. The sawdust on the floor was fresh. And the paintings on the wall above the gleaming mirrors behind the bar were suitably erotic, if one's tastes ran to overlarge breasts and hips wide enough to accommodate two at a time.

Striding up to the bar, Longarm waited for the barkeep, busy restocking his shelves, to take his order.

When the barkeep reached him, he ordered a beer. He took a few gulps past the suds, then wiped his lips with the back of his hand and asked the barkeep if he knew Dr. Dante.

"You mean Emile?"

"If that's his first name."

"You look healthy enough. Why would you want the doc?"

"That's my problem."

"It sure will be if you let that lush treat you."

"Drinks, does he?"

The barkeep stepped up and leaned over the bar to peer into the back of the saloon. He straightened up and stepped back down.

"Yeah, he's still at his table in the back there. You going down there to see him?"

"That's what I came in here for."

The barkeep reached down and pulled forth a bottle of unlabeled rotgut whiskey and slapped it onto the bar.

"All right then," he said. "Take this bottle down to him. The boss gave me orders not to let him go dry."

Longarm took the bottle, stepped back from the bar, and headed for the doc's table. The closer he got to the man, the more appalled he became. Slouched over the table, he resembled a skeleton some practical joker had dressed up in a scarecrow's outfit. He had an unkempt, scraggly Vandyke beard and, as Longarm noted when he sat down beside him, a pair of bloodshot, red-rimmed eyes.

"This is for you," Longarm told him, pushing the bottle toward him.

"Ah, yes," the doc said, pulling the cork and quickly filling his shot glass. "Good of you."

"Don't thank me. Thank the barkeep."

"You didn't bring a glass. Don't you drink?"

"I didn't want to crowd you. Looks to me like you need most of this."

"Real decent of you." The doc filled his shot glass again and slugged it down the hole. He looked Longarm over then and said, "You didn't come in here for a consultation, did you?"

"Yeah. I got a bad case of piles."

"Stop eating and stay out of the saddle."

"For how long?"

"Until you get rid of the piles."

"I might starve to death."

"What would you rather do, starve to death or die of piles."

"Neither."

"Drink plenty of beer. You'll piss a lot and you won't feel like eating. Best cure in the world for piles."

He poured himself another drink.

"The truth is," Longarm said. "I'm looking for a gent who might be in trouble."

"What kind of trouble?"

"Gunshot wound. Buckshot, to be more exact."

"Ah, yes." He downed another shot. He appeared almost alert now, perking up nicely.

"You know the gent?" Longarm persisted.

The doc nodded. "Dick Pratt."

"Yeah, that's him, all right."

"He a friend of yours?"

"Not exactly. He took a potshot at me."

"He won't take any more potshots at anyone."

"Why's that."

"His arm'll have to come off."

"Hurt that bad, eh?"

Dante nodded. "I'm going to see him later tonight. If he's still alive, I'll cut it off. No choice in the matter."

"Is he losing much blood?"

"Too damn much." The doc looked at Longarm shrewdly. "You're sure a big strapping son of a bitch. If you got piles, they must be as big as a buffalo's nuts. You wouldn't happen to be that U.S. deputy I been hearing about, would you?"

Longarm nodded. "Custis Long."

"I'm glad the forces of darkness have not yet caught up with you." He reached for the bottle. "Sure you won't join me? I hate to drink alone."

Longarm shook his head.

"So you're after the bastards who've been robbing the graves."

"I thought no one knew about it."

"The whole town does, but no one's talking out loud. Not to lawmen or strangers, anyway."

"You are right now."

"I'm a lush. Who listens to me."

"Where's Dick Pratt now?"

"At the Stockman's Rest."

"He alone?"

"He's with his sidekick. Birdie Lombard."

"You heard of John Thomaris."

"Yep. I heard of him."

"There's word going around that he's opening up an abandoned mine on Lookout Mountain. Do you believe that?"

"Hell, no. And nobody else does either."

The doc squinted unhappily at his bottle. It had lost its contents with astonishing speed.

"Well, now, look at that," he said, picking up the bottle and staring at it. "I'm running out."

Longarm left the table and walked over to the bar, caught the barkeep's eye, and indicated the doc with a nod of his head. The barkeep produced another bottle of rotgut and Longarm returned with it to the table and found the doc sound asleep, his face resting on the tabletop, a steady flow of urine dribbling down his pants legs onto the floor. Longarm took the bottle back to the barkeep and left the saloon.

Outside on the sidewalk he nearly ran over Miss Jean Langly.

"Oh, it's you!" she cried.

She was startled, but did not appear to be at all unhappy at sight of him.

"None other," Longarm said, doffing his hat. "And you're just in time to join me for dinner."

"Why, deputy," she said, taken aback, "are you quite sure?"

"I was never more sure of anything."

She laughed. "Where?"

"At the hotel."

"Do you recommend it?"

"I do."

"All right then."

She allowed him to slip his arm through hers,

and he proudly escorted her the two blocks to the hotel. After only a shadow of a noon meal—Eileen Turnbill's generous board allowed him little room for more—Longarm and Jean Langly lingered over their coffee while Longarm related what he had found so far. Then he prodded her for more details concerning her current assignment this far from New York.

"Have you ever heard of Alexander Turney Stewart?" she began.

"Should I have?"

"Well, possibly not out here. You might say he invented the department store. He was the third richest man in the country at the time of his death."

"And when was this?"

"Three years ago." She put down her coffee. "And I am *still* looking for the poor man's body."

"For who?"

"His widow. She's offering a twenty-five-thousand-dollars reward for the return of her husband's remains."

"Didn't she pay the ransom?"

"She paid, but the body was never returned."

"And you think it might be out here?"

"I followed a man to Golden. He was the chief caretaker of St. Mark's in the Bowery. That's where Stewart's body was taken from."

"What's his name?"

"John Thomaris."

"Go on."

"He's a very strange man. Do you know what his specialty is?"

"Tell me."

"He designs caskets, all kinds. All of them extremely costly. His work is very impressive, as are the few tombs he has already built."

"What a gruesome way to make a living."

"Yes," she said, shuddering. "It is not one I would choose."

"I been hearing about Thomaris. The word is he's in Golden to open up an abandoned mine."

She put down her coffee and leaned forward, her green eyes glowing with excitement. "An abandoned mine, did you say?"

He grinned back at her. "You heard me."

"My God, Custis, are you thinking what I'm thinking?"

"Yep. Which means I'd better get on my horse and take a ride out to Lookout Mountain."

"Alone?"

"Do you ride?"

"No. But I could hire a rig."

"Forget it."

She seemed slightly miffed at his curt dismissal, but protested no more, and they parted amicably in the hotel lobby a few minutes later.

He crossed the street to the livery and saddled up his rented mount and rode out of town. He was not more than a mile from Golden when he realized he had two riders on his tail. He was not surprised. Three miles farther on, he lifted into the hills and followed an old trace that cut between the towering flanks of weathered rocks and canyons, Lookout Mountain now dominating the sky ahead of him.

Pulling his mount to a halt in the shadow of a

canyon wall, Longarm glanced back. He did not have long to wait. Sunlight glinting off bits came clearly to him as the two riders crested a ridge and kept on down the trace toward him. They were making no effort to keep hidden, Longarm noticed, which meant they were either very sure of themselves—or just two men riding out like him to the Lodestone Mine.

Maybe it was both.

He turned his mount off the trace and headed into the badlands.

Boyd's two deputies pulled up.

"Looks like we'll have to go into that shit after him," Tucker said to his companion.

Of the two, Lem Tucker was the heavier and far more powerful, with a prominent beak of a nose and a gut that peeled over his gunbelt. His badge was pinned to a buttonless, black leather vest he wore over a red-checked shirt. A black, flat-brimmed Stetson sat on his untidy head.

Biddle moved unhappily on his saddle. He was a thin rail of a man with sunken cheeks and pale blue eyes. "He seen us ridin' behind him. We go in after him, he'll know for certain it's him we're following."

"He knows it already. He ain't that dumb. And what difference does that make anyway? It's two against one. What's the problem?"

"The problem is that's mean ridin' country. We could lose our horses easy in there. And this deputy marshal's a helluva tough man to bring down."

"You know that for sure, do you?"

"Ain't you heard of Longarm?"

"Sure I have."

"Well?"

"The thing is," Tucker said, patting his sixgun, "Longarm ain't heard of Lem Tucker."

"We better stay on the trace," Biddle said firmly. "We'll make better time, take up our positions near the mine entrance, and finish him. Boyd didn't say where we took him down, so long as we did it."

"You know for sure he's heading for the Lodestone, do you?"

"Where else would he be heading? By now he must've heard them rumors Thomaris spread. What better place to hide all them bodies?"

Tucker reflected a moment. "Yeah. You're right. Okay. We'll wait for him at the mine. Pick our own time and place."

Biddle chuckled. "That's just what I was thinking."

"Just so's we make sure it ain't *him* picks the time and place."

The two men booted their horses forward, keeping them to a steady, ground-devouring trot as they kept on the trace leading to the Lodestone Mine.

Longarm was disappointed. He had expected the two riders tailing him to follow him when he cut off the trace. Instead, they had paid no heed and kept on the trace. Now, expecting to see considerable activity at the mine entrance, he found nothing of the sort. This, he had figured, had to be the place to keep all those stolen bodies—a cool mine shaft reaching into Lookout Mountain.

But the place was as forlorn and undisturbed as any of the thousand abandoned mines scattered throughout the region.

He was lying on a ledge overlooking the entrance to the mine, his Winchester resting in front of him. Below the mine entrance he caught the rusted gleam of a corrugated steel roof still clinging to an old shack. And below it stretched the piles of slag that ran down the slope to the canyon floor. Ore cars and collapsed trestles, their twisted, rusted steel rails littering the slope, were the only reminders of the wealth that had been hauled from this mine shaft. Over it all hung rust and dust, the only sign of life the flocks of blackbirds wheeling up out of the canyon into the sky. Their raucous calls added to the air of complete abandonment that clung to the site. He had guessed wrong. He was not going to find any huge cache of expensive caskets hidden away inside the Lodestone Mine.

A rifle shot crackled from the rocks above him. The round chipped off a portion of the ridge near his right elbow. Another shot came from across the canyon. A bullet whined angrily off the rock wall behind him. A third shot came from above. This round came so close it whispered his name as it seared through the air inches from his right ear. He was not doing himself any good on this ledge, he realized, as a fourth round slammed into the ledge inches from his right boot. He jumped down onto a trail below the ledge and, hugging the mountain side, scuttled back into the rocks. He held up to take stock of his situation.

With him out of sight, the firing ceased. But that would not last. The two riflemen had him bracketed and were now just waiting for him to move his ass out of the hole he had just crawled into so they could finish him off. Longarm was fuming. Those two on the trace had not bothered to follow him into the badlands because they had known where he was heading. So they had gone ahead and set up this neat little trap.

And of course he had walked right into it.

You are getting soft, Mr. Long, he told himself. *And careless. Too much of the good life.*

He peeked out from behind the rock. Nothing. He stepped out and stood on the trail in full view. At once the fusillade began, the rifle fire coming as before from both sides of the canyon. He jumped back into cover and looked for a way to pick his way down the slope without leaving his cover. He edged carefully down the slope, moving swiftly across open spaces and only occasionally drawing fire. He was on the run, anxious to save his ass, and he didn't care who knew it.

A hundred yards or so from the canyon floor, he halted his downward flight, glanced up, and caught the gleam of sunlight on a rifle barrel poking out from behind a boulder. He swung up his rifle, crouched, and waited. A second later, the man holding the rifle stepped into sight—and into Longarm's sights.

Longarm squeezed off a shot. The man staggered back, dropping his weapon, then slumped out of sight.

Longarm scrambled quickly down the rest of the mountainside, then ran along the canyon floor to where he'd left his mount. It was gone. From the far side of the canyon a sudden fusillade opened up.

Cursing, he ducked back behind a boulder.

It was one-on-one now, but Longarm was still at a disadvantage. He was pinned down as neatly as a butterfly on a collector's board, and he had no horse, no way to escape this bastard's rifle fire. He would have to wait for dark and see what developed.

He became aware then of a rattle of wagon wheels plunging over the canyon's rocky ground. The clattering rattle—along with the pound of hooves—came rapidly closer. A farm wagon or maybe a rig. He heard the crack of a whip.

Around a bend in the canyon wall, a surrey with a fringe on top swept into view, Jean Langly driving the two-horse team.

What the hell?

He jumped out from behind the boulder, frantic.

"Get back!" he yelled. "Get out of here!"

Ignoring his cry, she leaned out over her horses and continued to sting their backs with her whip. The surrey swept closer.

Seeing she had no intention of going back, he left the canyon wall and ran toward her.

"Get out of here!" he pleaded. "There's a rifleman up there in the rocks!"

She stood up suddenly, her whip crackling like gunfire over the horses' back. The surrey rattled on toward him, bouncing recklessly over the rocky ground. He was surprised the surrey still had all its wheels.

"Stop yelling at me," Jean cried as she got close enough for him to hear her. "Get in!"

He was astounded at her foolhardy grit as she drove the team straight for him, the crack of her whip echoing like rifle fire in the narrow canyon. Nearing him, she began hauling back on the reins to slow the horses. Aware that this would make her a more inviting target, he redoubled his speed and ran straight for the surrey. She turned it slightly, enabling him to jump onto the seat beside her.

"Let's go!" he cried.

She smiled brightly at him. "Oh, you mean you don't want me to stop?"

He laughed. "You crazy? Keep going!"

She leaned forward, giving the team its head, urging them on with high, shrill cries. Longarm could tell she was really enjoying herself. He levered his Winchester and scanned the rocks above him, hoping to catch a glimpse of the other rifleman. For a brief moment he caught sight of a powerful figure standing on an outcropping of rock high above the canyon, a rifle held in his hand as he peered down at them. Sunlight glinted suddenly off a badge on his black leather vest. Then a great slab of rock came between them.

Longarm found it hard to believe—but there was no escaping the truth. Boyd, a fellow lawman, had sent his two deputies out here to kill him.

Lowering his rifle, he turned to face Jean Langly. "Where in the hell did you come from, Miss Langly?"

"Are you angry?"

"Hell, no. You just saved my ass."

"Good," she said, her whip snaking out over the

team's plunging backs. "That's something I wouldn't want you to lose."

"Oh?"

She glanced archly at him. "I have other plans for it."

Chapter 5

Boyd almost spilled his whiskey. "Dead? What the hell do you mean, dead?"

"I can't say it any clearer," said Tucker. "The round entered through Slim's guts and went out his neck."

"Jesus Christ."

"No. It was that U.S. deputy marshal. He got off a lucky shot."

Boyd tossed down his drink and slapped his glass onto the desk. "He's pretty damn lucky, that man."

"I could've finished him off."

"Well, why the hell didn't you?"

"I might've hit that new woman in town, the one from New York City. She came riding up in a surrey.

Before I could get a clear shot, the deputy jumped into it and she took off with him."

Boyd nodded in glum approval. "I saw her come in a little while ago. She was driving a team hauling a surrey. The deputy was on the seat beside her, and her team was lathered pretty good. It's a good thing you didn't chance firing at them. If you'd hit her, you would've raised a real stink."

"What I can't figure is what the hell she was doing out there."

"Daniel said she was in his place this morning. She's a private detective trying to track down a missing corpse. She's followed Thomaris all the way from New York."

Tucker grinned. "Well, now, ain't that something. And sure enough, it wasn't long before she'd heard about that mine he's supposed to be opening up out there."

"Yeah. Just like the deputy." Boyd shook his head in disappointment. "Dammit, Lem. You guys had him all to yourself out there. You could have finished him."

"Next time, Boyd, I'll get him."

"It may be too late now."

Boyd put his flask back into his drawer and slammed it shut. He had not offered Tucker a drink.

"So what do we do now?" Tucker asked.

"You mean what do I do? I'll handle this."

"Well, then. What're *you* going to do?"

Boyd got up. "I'm going over to see Walt and tell him we better wrap this thing up fast and get the hell out of here. What'd you do with Slim's body?"

"I left it for the buzzards. Not much on his bones, so it won't take long for him to be stripped clean."

"Yeah. I suppose that's one way to look at it."

A frown on his face. Boyd strode past Tucker and left the office. Tucker moved behind the town marshal's desk and took the whiskey flask out of the drawer, Boyd's glass, and unscrewed the flask. He poured himself a drink and threw it down. Since the son of a bitch had never seen fit to offer his own deputy a drink, Tucker felt no compunction at all in helping himself. He did so, in fact, at every opportunity. Soon now, this grave-robbing business would be done, Boyd would take off with his money, and Lem Tucker would be the next town marshal.

He poured himself a second drink and was placing the flask back into the drawer when he heard heavy footsteps, looked up, and saw the U.S. deputy marshal striding into the office.

"If you're looking for the town marshal, mister," the deputy said, shutting the drawer and stepping out from behind the desk, "he's over at the Last Chance."

"That so?"

"Yeah."

"Looks like you're the one got away," Longarm said.

"What the hell you talkin' about?"

"You don't recognize me, huh?"

"Why should I?"

"Well, I recognize you. I got a good glimpse of you. You were the son of a bitch shooting at me not too long ago at the Lodestone Mine."

"You're crazy. I don't know what you're talkin' about."

"Where's your buddy, the one I winged?"

The deputy shifted nervously under Longarm's relentless gaze. "I told you. I don't know what you're talkin' about."

"You mean you left the poor bastard out there for the buzzards to pick over?"

"Say, listen, lawman, you got no right to come in here and—"

"We ain't been introduced. How come you know I'm a lawman?"

"I heard tell you was in town," Tucker said lamely.

Longarm wanted satisfaction. He had been bushwhacked by this son of a bitch and his partner, and if a foolhardy—and very lovely—young lady had not come to his aid, he might still be back out in that canyon, maybe lying on his back with his mouth open and the ants moving in for a feast.

"Who sent you out there after me?"

"I told you. I don't know what the hell you're talking about. I been in town all day."

"What's your name, deputy?"

"Tucker. Lem Tucker."

"Tucker," he said evenly, "you're a goddamm liar."

Tucker swallowed but did not reply.

"And from the look of it, a coward as well."

Tucker's face darkened, but he managed to hold himself in check.

"You ready to tell me why Boyd sent you two assholes after me?"

"Look, Marshal, I ain't goin' to take no offense. You're makin' a mistake is all. Boyd didn't send me or anyone else after you."

"Maybe it was John Thomaris then."

Longarm caught the startled gleam in Tucker's eyes. Tucker sure as hell knew Thomaris, which meant the man from New York was definitely in on this ghoulish commerce.

"John ain't mixed up in nothing," Tucker replied, without too much conviction, "as far as I know."

"But you do know the man."

"Sure. Sure. I know him. What's that prove?"

"It proves you're in league with a known criminal," Longarm told the deputy. "He's wanted in New York in connection with a possible homicide."

"He's just an acquaintance, for Christ's sake!"

Smiling coldly, Longarm reached out and grabbed Tucker's vest and yanked him closer. Tucker's hat toppled off his head as he tried to wrest himself free by stepping back and ripping the vest from Longarm's grasp. Longarm only pulled him closer and with his left hand stripped the badge from his vest, then flung Tucker backward. The heel of Tucker's foot struck the wastebasket beside the desk, and he toppled backward to the floor, his head striking the wall with a mean thud.

His face suddenly livid with hate, Tucker went for his sixgun. Longarm waited until the iron cleared leather, stepped forward and kicked the gun out of his hand, hauled Tucker up onto his feet, and slammed him on the side of his head, sending him reeling backward into his boss's swivel chair. Then he picked up

Tucker's gun, emptied the cartridges onto the floor, and threw the gun at him.

"You're finished around here, Tucker," Longarm told him. "I'm willing to swear in a court of law you've associated with a known fugitive from the law and that you and your fellow deputy fired on me from ambush, attempted murder."

"Now, dammit, you got no proof of that!"

Longarm grinned at him. "Oh, yes I do. I saw you up on that ledge, Tucker, and will so testify in court. No use in you trying to deny any of this."

Tucker sat up in the swivel chair and dropped his empty gun into his holster. "I ain't admittin' nothing, you son of a bitch."

Longarm hauled Tucker onto his feet, belted him in the chops, and flung him back into the chair.

"You're getting too familiar, Tucker. Who gave you leave? I'm no friend of yours. Next time you address me, I want to hear the mister first."

Blood trickled from one of Tucker's nostrils and his upper lip had a crack in it and was beginning to swell. He lifted his arm and wiped off the blood with the back of his hand and swallowed hard. He watched Longarm warily, his eyes reflecting the black hatred he felt. His pride was sure as hell taking a beating—and Longarm felt a mean, uncharacteristic satisfaction.

Longarm leaned closer to the man and smiled meanly. "I'm lettin' you light out, Tucker. And if you're as smart as any rat in a sinking ship, you'll get out while you can."

Tucker's tongue moistened his cracked lip.

"And don't bother to say good-bye to Boyd," Longarm told him. "I'll be the one to tell him for you."

For a moment Longarm thought Tucker was going to square his shoulders and stand up to his bullying, tell him to go to hell. But that moment passed. Tucker sagged noticeably, then without a word pushed himself out of the chair, snatched his hat up off the floor, and scrambled past Longarm and out of the office.

Longarm followed after him and stood on the porch while Tucker made tracks for the livery stable. With one last furtive glance behind him, Tucker ducked into the livery. Not long after, his head bent as he rode out of the stable, he turned his horse down Main Street, lifted it to a lope, and headed out of town.

As soon as Tucker had vanished from sight Longarm stepped off the porch and headed across the street to the Last Chance.

When Boyd entered the Last Chance earlier, he had spotted Walt Kennedy at one of the poker tables in the rear. As Boyd got closer he saw that the gambler was, as usual, doing well.

A pile of chips sat in front of him while his inscrutable gaze scanned his cards. It was draw poker. Kennedy shoved his bet into the pot. As he did so he glanced up and saw Boyd. One glance at Boyd's face was enough to alert him. He straightened somewhat as he continued the game. The next go-around he did not draw, and a moment later he spread his hand faceup on the green felt. Full house. Ace high. The three other players threw down their hands in disgust.

Walt chuckled as he raked in his winnings.

"That's all, boys," he said. "I got business."

He stood up, swept the clattering chips into his hat, and walked over to the bar with Boyd. As soon as he had cashed in he put his hat back on and turned to Boyd.

"What is it?"

"Let's find a table."

Once they found one near the wall and sat down, Boyd said, "Slim's dead. That U.S. deputy marshal killed him."

"Son of a bitch. How'd it happen?"

Boyd relayed what Tucker had told him, then leaned back for Walt's response.

"Looks to me like we better close this operation up fast," Walt commented.

Boyd was relieved. "Just what I was thinking."

"I'll have to get hold of Thomaris."

"You think he'll go along?"

"He'll have to."

Turning about, Walt waved over Birdie Lombard. Birdie left the bar girl he was pawing—the ugliest girl Walt had ever hired—and hurried over.

"Go get John," Walt told him. "I want to see him pronto. Tell him I'll be upstairs."

"You want me to go right now?" Birdie was very disappointed.

"You heard me, Birdie," Walt snapped. "That wench won't be going anywhere."

With an unhappy nod, Birdie scurried from the saloon.

Boyd watched him go, then turned back to Walt. "We got anything coming up?"

"Just the Devlin corpse."

"When?"

"Tonight."

"Maybe we better forget it. Hell, ain't we pulled in enough yet?"

"That ain't the point. Thomaris has already set it up. It would be a pity to let this one go."

"That means we'll have to wait around for this widow to pay up. I heard she only got left the house and the clothes on her back."

"That ain't what Daniel says, and he knows her pretty well."

Boyd shrugged unhappily. There was nothing he could do about it then. This Thomaris was the brains of the operation, and he and Walt were working closely together.

"Look at it this way, Boyd," Walt explained patiently. "We need all we can get. It ain't just you we got to pay off, it's them three undertakers, too."

"Well, you can scratch Slim Biddle."

Walt got to his feet, a sardonic grin on his face. "Don't worry. I already took note of that. When I get through with Thomaris, I'll see you back at your office. And don't forget. We still got to deal with this deputy."

Boyd nodded, and was about to leave the saloon when he saw the U.S. deputy striding across the saloon toward their table.

"Speakin' of the devil," he said to Boyd under his breath. "Here comes the son of a bitch now."

Walt had already caught sight of the lawman. Pulling his chair back out, he slumped into it and waited with Boyd for the tall drink of water to reach them. Smoke was all but coming out of the U.S. deputy's ears, and after what Boyd had just told him, Walt did not have to guess why.

Longarm guessed that the gent who had just sat back down was the gambler Walt Kennedy, which meant he was up to his armpits in this ghoulish enterprise with Boyd.

He halted in front of them and tossed the badge he had torn off Tucker's vest onto the table in front of Boyd.

"Thought you might want this," he said.

Boyd picked it up, puzzled. "What the hell?"

"Tucker is gone. I sent him packing."

"You mean you fired him?"

"You could call it that."

"You got no right."

"I could have arrested him, charged him with attempted murder. I gave him a break."

"What the hell are you sayin'?"

"You know what I'm talking about. I don't like that kind of attention, Boyd."

"I don't know what the hell you're talkin' about, Long. Anything Tucker did, he did on his own."

"You're full of shit, Boyd. You want to, I'll make you eat it."

Then Longarm turned his attention to the gambler. "I figure you're in this with Boyd. So what I'm sayin' to him applies to you also."

"You must be chewing on loco weed, Marshal Long. I don't know what you're talkin' about."

"Play dumb if you want. But you're the one chewin' on loco weed if you keep up this ghoulish business of robbing graves and dunning widows for the return of their husband's remains. But I'm willin' to deal. Tell me where you're hiding them bodies, and I'll see the law goes easy on you."

Boyd and Walt Kennedy exchanged glances. Until that moment there had been a rising murmur from the saloon's astonished patrons as they watched the lone deputy marshal bracing Kennedy and Boyd. Now, however, there was a sudden, deadly silence as Longarm brought out into the open the whispered stories—and accusations—that must have been making the rounds for weeks.

The gambler shrugged and leaned back in his chair. "You must be crazy, deputy. You got no cause to come in here and accuse us of anything like that. All I do is run this saloon, and Boyd here wouldn't allow anything as crazy as what you just said in his town, would you, Boyd?"

"Damn right I wouldn't."

"As a lawman," Longarm said to Kennedy, "your friend here is a load of shit, and you're little more than a cheap, tinhorn gambler. It's a wonder you can bend your elbow with all them face cards up your sleeves."

A hush fell over the saloon as every man in it waited for the gambler's response to Longarm's measured insult.

Kennedy laughed nervously. "I know what you're trying to do, Long," he said. "You're trying to goad me, make me go for my gun. But I ain't goin' to let you call me out. There ain't no truth in what you said and everyone in this here saloon knows it." He smiled thinly. "And to show I ain't got no hard feelings, go on over to the bar. The drinks are on me."

"You know how you can always tell a coward, Kennedy?"

Kennedy did not respond.

"A coward can't be insulted."

Kennedy's smile remained, only it looked like it was pasted on.

Longarm turned his back on the two men, walked up to the bar, and told the barkeep to draw him a beer. Longarm drank it down casually, brushed his mouth off with the back of his hand, then strode from the saloon, not once looking back at Kennedy and Boyd.

Chapter 6

From the top of the backstairs, Longarm watched the doctor knock once on the door, then turn the knob and enter. Longarm left the stairwell, drew his sixgun and walked down the hallway, opened the door himself, and strode into the room.

Except for the doctor and the man lying on the bed, the room was empty.

"Well, now," said the doc, looking almost pleased to see Longarm. "You're just in time. Pratt here has been abandoned by his partner. So it looks like you'll have to stand in for him."

"Stand in for him?"

"Pratt's arm has to come off. I'll be needing your help."

Longarm dropped his .44 back into his cross-draw

rig, walked over to the bed, and looked down at the man resting on it, the same man, he realized, who had taken a potshot at him outside the widow Sanders's house.

"He don't look so hot, doc—not for an amputation."

"He ain't got no choice."

A tourniquet had been wound tightly around Pratt's arm just under his shoulder. It had stopped the bleeding, but obviously the loss of blood had been considerable. Pratt looked as pale as the filthy, bloody sheets he was lying on. But he was still breathing, and as the doctor peered down at him his eyes flickered open.

"Here we are, Dick," said the doc. "Goin' to fix you up."

"Hi, doc," Pratt managed. He lifted his head to look around the room. "Hey, where'd Birdie go?"

"Maybe he's at the Last Chance," said the doc. "You know what a thirst that man has."

"Son of a bitch. He just left me here."

"Was he the one put this tourniquet on your arm?"

"Yeah."

"Well, don't be so hard on him then. He saved your life."

"You goin' to sew me up now?"

"No, Dick. I'm going to amputate."

"Jesus, doc. Wait a minute. Wait a minute. Not so fast now."

"The quicker the better, Dick."

"No, doc. No!"

"Listen to me, Dick. Do you want to die?"

Pratt stared wide-eyed at the doctor, swallowed, then shook his head.

"All right then. Lay back down now and get yourself ready."

Pratt lay back down, cold sweat popping out on his forehead. Then came tears, pooling first in his eye sockets, then flowing down his cheeks. The man was terrified. But he was between a rock and a hard place, and he knew there was nothing he could do about it. As the doc busied himself ripping up sheets Longarm leaned close to Pratt.

"I need your help," he told him.

Pratt sobered somewhat as he turned his head to look up at Longarm. "What the hell kind of help?"

"Who's behind these kidnappings?"

Dick smiled, a wan but cocky smile. "Hell, we all are. Don't you know that yet, deputy?"

"By that you mean Walt Kennedy?"

"Hell, yes."

"And the undertakers?"

"Sure."

"And Boyd and John Thomaris?"

"Yeah. Yeah."

"Where are they taking all these bodies they've kidnapped?"

Pratt winced suddenly and closed his eyes. His torn-up arm was evidently still causing him considerable pain. "Nowhere," he muttered. "They ain't takin' them nowhere."

"Come on, Pratt!" Longarm demanded. "Tell me. Are they hidden inside a mine on Lookout Mountain?"

Pratt squinted up at Longarm through his pain. "Yeah," he rasped. "That's right. Out there. In one of them mines. Sure."

"Which one?"

"Christ, how the hell do I know?" Pratt said, his voice a barely audible groan by this time. "Leave me be, will you? I already told you all I know."

He let his head fall back onto the pillow and closed his eyes.

Longarm smelled chloroform and turned to see the doctor pouring it carefully onto a sponge from a small dark bottle. While Longarm had been questioning Pratt, the doctor had folded torn strips of bedsheet into absorbent packs to be used for sponging up the blood. Rolls of fresh white bandage he would need to wrap the stump had been taken from his bag and placed on the night table beside the bed. And close by the bed, ready to catch the arm when it fell, the doctor had set the chamber pot.

"Here," said the doctor, handing Longarm the saturated sponge. "Hold this chloroform over his nose. Just be careful you don't cut off his breathing."

"Jesus, doc," moaned Pratt. "Ain't there no other way?"

"Shut up, Dick," the doc responded coldly. "And lay still so we can get this over with. This ain't the first arm I've taken off."

With a feeble protesting cry, Pratt tried to sit up.

The doc nodded to Longarm, who pushed Pratt firmly back down onto the bed and pressed the sponge over his nose. For an instant longer Pratt struggled; then he sagged back and Longarm watched as his body gradually relaxed. Longarm glanced at the doctor. He was taking his hacksaw out of his black bag.

The doctor looked at Longarm. "Okay. You can lift off the sponge now," he said. "Pratt's out."

Longarm lifted the sponge. The strong fumes caused his head to reel momentarily.

"Hold it away from you," the doctor told him.

Longarm nodded and put the sponge down next to the lamp on the nightstand.

"Be ready to grab that sponge if he comes out of it."

Longarm nodded.

"Ready?"

"As ready as I'll ever be."

"Rest your hands on his shoulder. Steady him while I use this saw. I promise I won't take long."

"Do it then."

The doctor touched the saw to the flesh about six inches from the shoulder, then dug in with a will. Longarm looked away as the blood spurted. True to his word, the doctor cut through the bone with astonishing speed. The shattered arm dropped to the chamber pot, clattered off its side, and brushed his instep as it rolled partway under the bed.

The doctor put down the saw and, taking up his scalpel, began slitting the skin behind the stump, then peeled the skin back from the stump for at least two inches. He picked the saw back up and cut through the bone without touching the skin flap. As the bloody piece of bone splashed into the chamber pot, the doc pulled the skin flap back down over the stump, snatched up one of the absorbent packs, and held it firmly against the stump in an effort to stem the flow of blood. But almost immediately the blood soaked through it.

"Here," said the doctor to Longarm. "Hold this against the stump as tight as you can get it. I've got to cauterize the stump yet."

Longarm snatched up another absorbent cloth and did his best to staunch the flow of blood while the doc lifted the chimney off the lamp and rested a broad knife blade in the flame. The blade smoked, then began to glow. When the doc deemed it hot enough, he lifted it from the flame and nodded to Longarm.

Longarm pulled away the cloth. The doctor moved swiftly, thrusting the blade against the stump, then gliding it swiftly over the bloodied muscle tissue, nerves, and veins surrounding the bone. The stench of burning flesh filled the room, that and the hiss of the blade as it turned blood to steam. It took three more similar applications of the doctor's knife to finish cauterizing the stump. Then, with amazing swiftness, the doctor sewed the skin flaps around the blackened stump and then tied a snug bandage around it.

The doc stepped back and waited. When no blood showed through the fresh white bandage, he turned and grinned wearily at Longarm.

"Now you know why they call a doctor a sawbones."

"I always knew, doc."

"How do you feel?"

"Not so good."

"I don't blame you. I feel rather poorly myself."

The room resembled a charnel house. A large stain of blood discolored the wallpaper beside Longarm.

Longarm remembered vaguely when the blood had gouted past him the instant the doc's saw had bitten into flesh. The floor was black and sticky with blood. The discarded arm was still half under the bed, the smaller stump bobbing in the slops jar.

The doc frowned suddenly and stepped closer to peer down at Pratt's face.

"What's the matter?" Longarm asked.

Without answering, the doc leaned over and rested the back of his hand against Pratt's carotid artery. A moment later, straightening up, he reached into his black bag and took out his stethoscope. Inserting the prongs into his ears, he began searching for a heartbeat.

In a few moments he gave it up. Pulling the stethoscope from his ears, he flung it wearily into his bag. "The son of a bitch didn't make it."

Longarm frowned down at Pratt. "All that for nothing."

The doctor picked up the sponge and held it to his nose for a second. "Maybe I poured on too much chloroform. I just didn't want him to feel anything."

His face grim, the doc dropped his bloody saw—bits of pale flesh still clinging to its teeth—back into his bag, placed the rolls of bandage beside it, then dropped in the still-saturated sponge and closed the bag.

"I need a drink," the doctor told Longarm. "Let's get the hell out of here."

When he reached the lobby, the doc walked over to the front desk and told the night clerk that there was a dead body in room 204.

"Jesus, doc! What are you saying?"

"Dick Pratt is dead," the doc explained wearily. "And the room will need a good scrubbing down, too."

"My God, what happened?"

"I had to take off Dick Pratt's arm. He didn't survive. Simple as that."

The desk clerk—a small, bald-headed fellow dressed in a neat dark suit, white shirt, a black string tie knotted at his throat—sighed deeply as he finally accepted the doc's explanation.

"You want me to call an undertaker, doc?"

"That would be a good idea."

The clerk said, "I'll call O'Brian's."

"All right. Tell him I'll be over tomorrow morning to sign the death certificate."

The doc turned and led Longarm out into the night. Pausing on the Cattleman Rest's porch, he looked gloomily at Longarm. "You goin' to join me?"

"Not tonight, doc."

"Did Dick tell you anything that might help?"

"I won't know for sure until I check it out. He sure as hell didn't give me much."

"Oh, I wouldn't say that."

The doc descended the steps and disappeared into the street's gloom on his way to the Last Chance. He had been cold sober through all this and was obviously in a hurry to remedy that condition.

And Longarm didn't blame him.

"You don't look very good," Jean said, answering his knock.

"I don't feel so good either."

She reached out and took his arm. "Come in, come in," she said, pulling him inside. "Tell me what happened."

Longarm started to speak, then found himself staring. She had combed out her long blond hair so that it spilled onto her shoulders. She was wearing only a cloudlike negligee, its filmy evanescence leaving nothing to his imagination, from the proud, assertive swell of her pink-nippled breasts to the glowing splendor of her blond pubic hair. A robe hung on the bedpost, but seemingly unaware of her negligee's effect on him, she made no effort to put it on.

"Tell me," she said. "What happened?"

He sat down on the edge of the bed and told her how Dick Pratt had died. And his adventures earlier goading the lions in their den and sending Lem Tucker packing.

When he finished, Jean took off his hat and frock coat and hung them up in her closet. He watched her walk to the closet and back. Then he grinned weakly at her and asked if she would mind putting on a robe or something.

"You don't like my negligee!" she cried with a pout. "But you must. It's from Paris, and this is the first time I've worn it since New York! Don't you like it? Really?"

She spun about in front of him, enabling him to take in her figure's every voluptuous line.

"I like it fine," he admitted.

"And you like what it encloses."

"Of course."

"I saved your life this afternoon. Have you forgotten?"

"No, I haven't."

"So now you must return the favor. You must save my life."

"What are you talking about?"

"I am starved for affection. I need you to keep me alive. Such hungers I have, Custis! I am consumed by them. It is spring, and I want to fly."

She sat down on the bed beside him. Her hand dropped to his thigh and squeezed gently. Then she laughed softly and rested her head on his shoulder.

"Will you help me fly?"

"Fly, eh? That's one way to put it."

Her fingers moved softly up his inner thigh. His crotch came to attention.

"You know, Custis," she told him softly, "we women want the same thing men do—and for the same reason."

"I'd just about figured that out," he replied.

She reached down and with her other hand unbuckled his pants. "Well, then," she said. "Come ahead and rescue me."

"I'm not really in the mood, Jean."

"Oh, I'll take care of that. I will seduce you."

With a sigh, he lay back on the bed and let Jean have her way with him.

After she had her way with him, he sat up on the edge of the bed and stared out through the window at the black night.

"Sorry about that," he said.

"Why, what for, Custis? You did fine—just fine. For any normal woman, I'm sure your performance would have been more than sufficient. Unfortunately, I am afraid I cannot be classified as normal. I am insatiable, rather."

Longarm turned his head to look at her, bemused. No woman that was a real woman was anything but insatiable. He wondered what made her think she was so different. He glanced back out the window.

"Next time," she said, "we can spend a little more time. We'll be better acquainted by then."

"You're being very understanding."

"No problem, Custis. You're spent. I'm resigned. I'll just have to wait for you to recover."

He laughed without any resentment and found himself recalling Eileen Turnbill. Which promptly caused him to think of something. He got up from the bed and went over to the chair over which Jean had tossed his pants and fished in the pocket for the obituary he had torn from Eileen Turnbill's copy of the local paper. Unfolding it, he read it, then passed it across the bed to Jean.

She read it, then handed it back to him, immediately interested. "Do you think this woman—this Annie Devlin—is going to have her husband's remains taken also?"

"What do you think?" he asked.

"I don't know what to think. But surely they wouldn't try to kidnap this widow's husband now—now that they know you're onto them."

"I just wanted to push them into a foolish move.

And if they're going to pull out, how could they resist making this last snatch before they do?"

"So what are you going to do?"

"Stake out the funeral parlor. If they make off with the body, I'll follow—"

"And find out where they've taken the others!" she finished, delighted with his plan.

"That's the idea."

"Do you know where O'Brian's Funeral Parlor is?"

"No. But it shouldn't be hard to find."

"I can tell you where it is. I've already visited the place. It's two blocks behind the livery on a side street near the stream. It's not the most luxurious of funeral parlors, Custis."

"That figures. It's where the doc sent Dick Pratt's body."

Longarm reached for his long johns.

Watching him step into them, she said, "You won't let me come with you, I suppose."

"I'd prefer not, Jean."

She sat back against the headboard and folded her arms. She had helped him strip, but now she let him dress all by himself. He could tell she was a little disgruntled at not being asked to go along, but he knew also that she understood perfectly why this was no job for her.

At the door he turned. "Good night, lovely lady."

"Please, Longarm," she said. "Be careful." Then she grinned impishly. "And don't tire yourself unduly."

Longarm found O'Brian's Funeral Parlor with little difficulty. Behind it an alley ran parallel to a dry stream bed. He stepped into the shadows of a warehouse and kept his eyes on the funeral home's wide, double-door rear entrance.

More than an hour later he was still in the shadows, beginning to wish he was back in Jean's bed, when a block farther down a flatbed wagon pulled by two draft horses rattled into the alley. It kept coming until it pulled up in front of the funeral home's rear entrance, and a man Longarm did not recognize jumped down. The funeral parlor's rear door opened and a small redheaded individual in dark trousers and a gleaming white shirt and black tie—most likely O'Brian, the funeral director—stepped into the alley, looked up and down, then satisfied it was empty, followed the wagon driver into the building.

It was not long before the funeral director reappeared in the funeral parlor's rear entrance. Again he looked up and down the alley, then beckoned quickly to someone behind him. The driver of the wagon appeared, holding one end of a canvas bag that carried the recently deceased body of Annie Devlin's husband. Behind him, holding the body's head and shoulders, was a fellow dressed in a tweed suit, derby hat, and tie—obviously John Thomaris, the man Jean had followed out here. Because of the darkness Longarm could not be sure, but it appeared there was a toothpick in the corner of his mouth.

The undertaker unhitched the wagon's tailgate and stepped aside. The two men turned, lifted the body and shoved it onto the wagon's bed, then stepped back. The driver lifted the tailgate and Longarm could hear the clank of the heavy chains as he secured it.

After a few words with John Thomaris, the driver climbed up onto the seat, unwrapped the ribbons from around the brake lever, and gave the team its head. The undertaker watched the wagon rattle off, waited until it cleared the alley, then walked back into his funeral parlor and closed the door, leaving Thomaris alone in the alley. Sticking a fresh toothpick into his mouth, John Thomaris strode down the alley and a moment later disappeared into the shadows.

Longarm was depressed to see how easily—even casually—this grisly abduction had been accomplished. For these bastards, it was like having a license to steal. And now the widow Devlin would get a note from the kidnappers demanding what little money she had left after the death and funeral services of her husband.

Stepping from the shadows, Longarm hurried down the alley. His intention was not to overtake John Thomaris, but to get a horse from the livery and follow that wagon.

Chapter 7

At the livery, Longarm found the roan he had rented from the Diamond K stamping restlessly in one of the stalls. He asked the hostler about it and was told the roan had returned on its own that afternoon, lathered and just a mite spooked. Longarm flipped the oldtimer a coin for his trouble, saddled the roan, and rode out.

In the bright moonlight he had no difficulty picking out the wagon in the distance. He left the trace and kept to the high ground, staying well back as he followed the flatbed. At first it looked as if Devlin's corpse was on its way to the Lodestone Mine; at the last minute, however, the driver turned south off the trace, and soon Lookout Mountain's great-shouldered heft loomed on his right, filling the night sky and blocking out the moon. Without the moon's bright wash to guide him, Longarm found it difficult to keep up with the wagon in the high, broken ground, and he was forced to go back onto the trail the wagon driver was using.

He kept well back, and an hour or so later the flatbed pulled up alongside a shack perched between two enormous slag heaps below an abandoned mine. Longarm smiled grimly. He had been on the right track all along. They were using a mine to cache their bodies, only it was not the Lodestone, but this other, less well known mine. The entrance to it was barely visible about a hundred yards farther up the slope.

He could tell little else in the darkness. He dismounted and led his horse off the trail into a gully and tethered it to some scrub brush, then proceeded closer on foot, his rifle at the ready. By the time he reached the cabin, the flatbed driver was inside it. A light flared in the cabin as the man lit a lantern. Longarm could barely make out the man through the single begrimed window.

He crouched down and waited for the man to return to the wagon for Devlin's corpse. He wanted to catch the man red-handed, then check out the mine, take the fellow back to Golden, and corral the others—including the three morticians. Whoever this driver was, his testimony would clinch the case. This time, it appeared, Vail was right. It hadn't taken long at all.

The door to the shack opened and the flatbed driver stepped out. He was carrying the lantern with him to light his way back to the wagon—and up to the mine also, Longarm figured. As the driver passed close by him Longarm got a whiff of him. It was powerful enough to turn back a charging bull buffalo. Just the sort of gent you'd want transporting dead bodies.

Longarm followed carefully after him, keeping well back. He didn't want to pass out this early in the game. Crouching behind a boulder, he watched the man unchain the tailgate. As soon as he reached in for the body Longarm stepped out of his cover and walked boldly toward the wagon, making no effort to be quiet.

Hearing his footsteps, the wagon driver turned. Longarm aimed the rifle at the man's midsection.

"Don't try anything stupid," Longarm advised him.

But the fellow showed no alarm or even surprise at Longarm's sudden appearance. Instead, he smiled, his yellow teeth gleaming in the darkness.

"Don't you worry none, mister," he drawled. "I ain't goin' to try nothin' stupid. You already took the prize for that."

A boot heel crunched into the gravel behind him and Longarm realized he had been suckered. Someone rammed the barrel of a sixgun into the small of his back. A hand reached around and snatched the rifle from his grasp, then tossed it at the fellow standing by the wagon.

Lem Tucker stepped around in front of Longarm. "Been waiting out here for you, Long. Walt was right. He knew you'd be tracking this body. You sure as hell are an easy man to reel in."

"Go ahead, Lem," said the wagon driver eagerly. "Give him a pasting, why don't you?"

"Shut up, Birdie," Tucker said. "I'll handle this."

Tucker lifted Longarm's .44 out of his rig, then stepped back and swung the sixgun, catching Longarm smartly on the side of his head. Lights exploded inside his skull, and when he regained his senses, he was on his ass looking up at the two men. The one called Birdie stepped forward and kicked him in the right side. Longarm absorbed the punishment with a grunt, but when Birdie tried to do it a second time, he caught the man's foot with both hands and twisted it. Squealing, Birdie toppled backward to the ground.

"You hurt my ankle!" he cried as he scrambled hastily to his feet and limped out of Longarm's grasp.

Tucker chuckled meanly. "Serves you right, you stupid son of a bitch," he told Birdie.

Longarm got to his feet.

"Turn around," Tucker told him.

Longarm did so and Tucker shoved him roughly toward the wagon and onto the flatbed. Longarm tried to sit up but was pushed facedown and found himself lying alongside Devlin's corpse. Birdie clambered up into the wagon and sat beside Longarm, poking the barrel of Longarm's rifle into his side, his stench hanging so close that Longarm made no effort to sit up again. He preferred the corpse.

Tucker got up on the wagon's seat and drove the team up a steep, winding grade that led to the mine entrance. When they got there, Tucker ordered Longarm to help Birdie carry Devlin's body into the mine shaft. With Birdie holding a lantern for light, his left arm wrapped around the body's legs, and Tucker at the rear to keep an eye on Longarm, they entered the mine shaft and went in deep, past rotting timbers and through pools of water that at times completely covered Longarm's ankles.

At last they reached a tool and storage area cut out of the rock. With his shoulder Birdie pushed open the sagging door and Longarm followed him. On all sides Birdie's lantern revealed the shadowy forms of abandoned equipment, shovels, picks, wheelbarrows, most of them apparently rusted out or broken.

"Okay," said Tucker, following them in. "This is far enough."

Birdie promptly let go of the body's feet. Longarm let go, too, then stepped back as the dead body slammed to the damp ground. In the lantern's dim light Longarm glanced quickly around, looking for the other bodies he had expected to find. But he didn't see a one.

Watching him, Lem Tucker chuckled. "What're you lookin' for, lawman? Ghosts?"

Longarm didn't reply. He had been suckered from the beginning, it looked like. This might have been a fine place to stash the bodies, but they sure as hell weren't here.

"Thought you'd find all them bodies we kidnapped, didn't you?"

"Yes," Longarm admitted.

"Well, don't worry. There'll be two bodies here soon enough."

As he spoke he flipped off the rifle's safety, stepped closer, and poked Longarm with the barrel. It was obvious what he had in mind.

Suddenly Birdie screamed.

Longarm turned to see him pointing at Devlin's dead body, his eyes wide in sheer terror. And for good reason. The body wrapped in the dark army blanket was moving! Then a hand reached out and flung aside the blankets covering him.

"My God, he's comin' back to life!" Birdie cried, dropping his lantern.

Hitting the floor, the lantern's chimney clattered, the kerosene flared for an instant, then winked out as the wet floor diluted it. In the sudden darkness, Longarm grabbed the rifle barrel, pushed it away from his gut, then yanked it from Tucker's grasp. The rifle discharged. Birdie howled in sudden pain.

"I'm hit!" he cried. "Jesus, I'm hit."

The darkness was total—there was no hint of light or of shadow. Nevertheless, Longarm cranked in a fresh cartridge and fired at the spot where he thought Tucker was, but he missed and a second later he heard the man at the door. He levered and fired blindly again. The door creaked open, then closed, and a second later Longarm heard Tucker wedge a beam against it.

Longarm rushed to the door and flung his shoulder against it. With the beam wedged solidly against it, the door gave only slightly. Behind him Birdie was thrashing on the floor, moaning in pain. Longarm again flung himself at the door. And then someone was beside him, hurling himself at the door also.

Devlin's corpse wanted out, too.

"Hey, what's going on!" Devlin's corpse cried. "Am I dead, or what? Why is it so dark in here?"

Longarm stepped back from the door, amazed. The man standing beside him was not the widow Devlin's husband, but a resurrected Dick Pratt.

Behind them on the floor, Birdie cried out, "Hey, that you, Pratt?"

"Yeah. It's me."

"Shit, we thought you was dead!"

"Well, I ain't—but goddammit, my arm's gone but I can still feel it."

"How bad you hurt, Birdie?" Longarm asked him.

"Bad. Real bad. You got me in the gut, you bastard."

Following the sound of Birdie's voice, Longarm knelt by him. Birdie's stench was overpowering, but Longarm paid no heed as he lifted the man's sixgun from its holster.

"You won't be needin' this, Birdie."

"You goin' to leave me here, you bastard?"

Without replying, Longarm returned to the door, nearly running into Pratt in the complete darkness.

"Okay, Pratt," Longarm told him. "When I say go, ram the door as hard as you can. Ready?"

"Go ahead."

Longarm gave the signal, but the two of them did not hit the door in unison and it gave hardly an inch.

"Come on, Pratt," Longarm urged. "We got to do this together. Try it again."

The next effort was better, and on their third rush one rotted plank gave way. It was shoulder-high, and Longarm reached down through the opening, grabbed the beam wedged against the door, and dislodged it.

The door swung wide. Pratt brushed past Longarm. He could hear Pratt running down the mine shaft toward the entrance.

Longarm went back and tried to rouse Birdie, but the man was now unconscious. Longarm slapped the ground until he found his rifle, then followed after Pratt, running his hand along the side of the mine shaft to give him direction. Ahead of him Pratt cursed as he stumbled and fell repeatedly in his wild eagerness to escape this awful darkness. Longarm gained on him steadily, but it was the one-armed Pratt who broke out of the mine first, his body lurching out into the cool night.

A shot rang out.

Pratt crumpled and cried out to Tucker, but a second shot cut off this cry. He vanished from sight. Longarm dropped to the floor of the mine shaft, then elbowed his way to the entrance, pushing his rifle ahead of him, and peered out at the cool night and the flatbed wagon sitting on the narrow dirt road in front of the mine shaft.

From behind the flatbed a rifle cracked. The bullet whined past Longarm and thudded into a support beam. Aiming at the powder flash, Longarm squeezed off two quick shots, then hugged the ground as Tucker's return fire whined close over his head. A second later he heard the wagon start up.

Jumping up, Longarm ran out of the mine and managed to overtake the wagon before it could get up any speed. Pulling himself onto the wagon bed, he hung on as the wagon slewed around to make the first cutback. Tucker knew he was in the wagon and managed to throw a slug at him. But his aim was lousy, and before he could fire again, Longarm hit him with full force and they both went tumbling off the wagon seat.

They hit the slope with numbing force, and when Tucker tried to scramble away, Longarm brought him down with a tackle from behind. For a moment they struggled beside the halted team, exchanging feeble, awkward punches, until Tucker managed to scramble back out of Longarm's clutches and get off a shot. Missing Longarm, the bullet ricocheted off one of the draft horse's traces. The horse whinnied and reared. Longarm turned, saw the horses bolt toward him, and flung himself out of their path.

Tucker was not so lucky.

He slipped as he ducked aside and went down in front of the charging team. The horses thundered over him. His muffled cry was cut off as the pounding hooves cut him to pieces. Reaching his dismembered body, Longarm saw at once that Tucker was gone. He went back to the mine entrance—and found Dick Pratt with two bullets in him. He was dead for sure this time.

Longarm dragged his dead body into the mine, then went after Tucker's body and dumped him beside Pratt.

A few hours before dawn Longarm rattled into Golden, his roan tied to the wagon's rear. He left the wagon in front of O'Brian's Funeral Parlor, untied his roan, and rode back to the livery. Without awakening the hostler, he off-saddled the horse, crossed the street to the hotel, and went up to his room. He pulled off his boots, lay back, and was asleep almost instantly.

A sharp, peremptory rap on his door awoke him.

He sat up and drew his .44. It was daylight. Sunlight was pouring in through the window, bright enough to give him a headache.

"Who is it?"

"Jean."

Longarm got up from the bed and opened the door. Jean stepped quickly into his room and closed the door. Then she looked him up and down. "You look awful. What happened?"

Longarm walked back to the bed and sat down on it and told her.

"That poor man Pratt," Jean said. "After going through all that . . ."

"Crazy business, all right. If he hadn't come back from the dead when he did, I wouldn't be here now."

"Then you're certain it was a trap?"

"No doubt of it, and they baited it with Pratt's body. He wasn't worth burying, so they used him as a piece of cheese—and I went for it."

"So what now?" she said, sitting down on a wooden chair next to the bed.

He took a good look at her. She was wearing the same dress she had worn when he met her in the undertaker's reception room two days before. She looked as fresh and exciting now as she had then. All he hoped was she didn't ask him to prove it—not right then, at any rate.

"I'm not sure," he replied.

"Why don't you arrest Boyd?"

"On what charge?"

"His deputies tried to kill you, didn't they?"

"What proof do I have they weren't acting on their own?"

"You know they weren't."

"Sure. But what's my proof?"

"What about the undertakers? You know they've been acting as middlemen for the kidnappers. O'Brian especially. You saw him with Thomaris."

"They could all claim they had no choice. They were just following orders. And they could claim the reason they kept quiet was to prevent the kidnappers from destroying the bodies. In other words, they were acting on behalf of the widows."

Jean sighed. "You're right. No one would argue with that. Look how quiet every bereaved widow has kept these past weeks. No one has uttered a peep, except for Tom Sanders's widow."

"And Eileen Turnbill."

"So even though you know who's behind this, you can't do anything?"

"I just need to keep boring in on them. Wait for a mistake. What can you tell me about this gent you followed from New York?"

"I think Thomaris is the brains of this gang, Custis. And he's operating just as he did in New York. He keeps out of sight. It's almost like he's invisible. But I know for sure he's staying upstairs in Kennedy's apartment over the saloon."

"Does he know you're in Golden?"

"Oh, yes. He's seen me . . . twice, as a matter of fact."

"What was his reaction?"

"A polite bow and a supercilious smile. He's aware of how little I know, I am afraid."

"I only caught a glimpse of him at O'Brian's. But it looked to me like he was in charge, all right."

"We could kidnap him," Jean suggested. "Force him to tell us where the bodies are."

He looked at her in surprise. "You mean *force* it out of him?"

"Why not?"

"Well, that isn't exactly legal, you know. And he'd know that and keep quiet. Unless, of course, you broke off one of his arms."

She shuddered, her face growing pale. "*Really,* Custis!"

"Well, then. I reckon we can forget about that option."

"What *can* you do?"

Longarm said nothing for a while. "Keep the pressure on, force them to make a mistake."

"And that's all?"

"Yes."

"Am I included?"

"Sure. But not right now."

He lay back on the bed and closed his eyes. He was weary of all this palaver. He heard Jean's dress rustle as she got to her feet.

"I presume I have been dismissed," she said.

He opened his eyes and peered at her. "I only got in a few hours before dawn," he explained. "I need more sleep."

"No need to explain," she told him. "Remember? I'm resigned. And you're spent—all wrung out."

As soon as she closed the door Longarm got up and pulled on his boots. He was heading for the door when he held up and unclipped his derringer from its chain and tucked it down into the back of his right boot. He stomped a moment to get it comfortable, then lifted his watch out of its pocket and placed it in the top dresser drawer.

Then he left the hotel.

"I say arrest the son of a bitch," said Kennedy. "Put him behind bars."

"It won't stick," Boyd said.

He had just returned from the mine and had found the three bodies. He had been unable to explain why Dick Pratt's body had been found alongside Tucker's torn and broken remains inside the mine entrance.

"Why not?" Walt asked.

"He's a lawman, a federal officer. He'll be out in a matter of days. And we'll be stickin' our necks out."

"Our necks are already out. Way out. This son of a bitch's got to be stopped—slowed down, at least."

"Well, maybe I got a way," Boyd said.

"Well, if we can't arrest him, what the hell can we do?" Thomaris asked.

"Kill him."

"We already tried that," Walt reminded him.

"I admit it. It's my fault we messed up. I gave the job to a couple of assholes."

"So?"

"Let me handle it this time."

"You?"

"Yes, me."

"How you going to do it—and keep it quiet?"

"I have a little ace in the hole. Cute little thing. And she's scared enough to want Long out of this as much as we do."

"Who's that?" Thomaris asked.

"That's my little secret."

"No games, Boyd," Walt said. "If you got a way to get that son of a bitch out of our hair, do it. We ain't got much time."

"See you, gents," Boyd told them, heading for the door.

As soon as it had closed behind the town marshal, Walt looked at Thomaris. "You think he can do it?"

"He goddamn well better."

Walt nodded. *Amen to that,* he thought. The carpet-bags filled with bank notes in the other room were ready to go—and so was he. But they wouldn't be getting a single bank note out of Golden with that big, creepy son of a bitch poking his nose into every little corner.

Chapter 8

Mrs. Annie Devlin was in her late fifties, a plump, rosy-cheeked woman with beautiful large brown eyes. But the flesh around her eyes was still puffy from too much crying, and Longarm did not like disturbing her. She finished bringing in the tea tray, and pouring Longarm's and her own tea, offered him some tiny biscuits. He took one, sat back on her living-room sofa, and apologized for the second time for disturbing her.

"Now, don't you fret, deputy Long," she said. "I been sitting here for too long thinking on Charlie's death. It's about time I had someone to visit me. It'll do me good."

"That's very kind of you." He sipped his coffee and wondered how to begin.

He didn't have to. Annie Devlin started for him.

"I know why you're here, deputy. It's about these terrible kidnappings."

"Yes."

"They told me not to tell anyone, but I don't care. I am simply furious at such people. How could anyone be so cruel?"

"That's a good question. Have you already received a ransom note?"

"Yes, I have," she said bitterly.

"Do you mind my asking how much they want?"

"Two thousand dollars, deputy."

"Do you have it?"

"I have the money now. I mortgaged my home. But how I'll pay off the mortgage I have no idea."

"Who are you supposed to give it to?"

"Mr. O'Brian."

"When?"

"Today. Later today."

"I got here just in time then."

She put her teacup down, alarmed. "Oh, my. You mean you aren't going to let me give the money to them?"

He smiled quickly to allay her alarm. "No, I don't mean that. I have no intention to stop you. Do you have the money here in the house?"

"Yes, I do."

"Is it in bank notes or gold?"

"Bank notes."

"Good. Could I see it?"

"Yes," she said uncertainly. "I suppose so."

"Perhaps we could go into the kitchen?"

"The kitchen?"

"I would like a table to work on—and a safety pin."

"A table? And a safety pin?"

He laughed. "I'm not crazy," he assured her.

"Well, of course you aren't," she said, getting to her feet. "Come along, deputy. The kitchen's in here."

As soon as he was comfortable at the kitchen table she vanished out the kitchen door. He waited awhile, heard a barn door slam shut, and a moment later she reappeared with a large shoe box.

"I hid the money in the chicken coop out back," she explained, blushing.

He took the box from her and dumped the bank notes onto the table. There were twenty crisp one-hundred-dollar bills.

"Could I have that safety pin?" he asked the widow.

"Oh, yes. Of course."

She vanished into a small room off the living room and returned with a small round tin box. Opening it, she produced a large safety pin and handed it to him. Then she sat down to watch him, more than a little curious.

"I'm going to mark these bills," Longarm told her. "When we pack these animals in, this will be proof positive that they extorted you."

"Oh," she said, her voice tiny as she watched.

Longarm worked swiftly, pricking two holes adjacent to each other on the upper-right-hand border of each bank note. It took a while. He was very careful not to make a mess of it. He didn't want the holes to be caught by the kidnappers. After a few minutes, the widow brought in his teacup and saucer and poured him a second cup of tea, stirring in his cream and honey.

When he had completed his task, he placed the bills back in the shoe box and leaned back.

"You can bring the money in to O'Brian now," he told her.

"Mr. Long, do you think Mr. O'Brian is a part of this?"

Longarm debated the wisdom of telling her what he thought. If he told her he thought O'Brian and the others were tied up in these kidnappings, it might make her too angry—or upset—to give O'Brian the money calmly. She might even let it slip that the money was marked.

"I don't think so, Mrs. Devlin. He's probably as upset about all this as you and the rest are. When you give him the money, I suggest you say as little as possible. Be best for both of you."

"Oh, you needn't worry about me, Marshal. I won't let on a thing. You can can count on me."

"Fine. And if things go well, maybe we can get this money back and you can repay your mortgage."

Longarm got up from his chair and put on his hat and let the little plump woman show him out.

Michael J. O'Brian was a graying, overdressed man in his late fifties with the ruddy, veined nose of a man accustomed to the bottle and sharp, calculating brown eyes. Longarm had just shown the man his badge and told him he wanted to make sure the widow Devlin's dead husband had indeed been kidnapped.

"You say you are acting on behalf of Mrs. Devlin?" O'Brian asked warily.

"That's what I said."

"Seems like a crazy thing. Don't she believe her husband's been kidnapped?"

"She does, but I'm just a little curious about that."

With a shrug the man said, "Follow me."

He led Longarm into a damp cellar, down a long passageway that led into what appeared to be huge icebox with massive coffins lined up on both sides, all of them on wheeled platforms. Some of the caskets were more garish than others, brass handles and fittings gleaming in the dim, fitful lantern light—but all of them had the ponderous weight of death attached to them. It was a somber, even chastening experience. Longarm had never seen so many dead people waiting to be buried in his life and shivered involuntarily.

O'Brian stopped at a casket emblazoned with the dead man's name on a small brass nameplate, pulled it out on its platform, and lifted the lid. The coffin's white satin interior—bereft of its overdressed and waxen-faced occupant—gleamed and shimmered in the lamp's flickering light. After a quick glimpse into the empty casket, Longarm nodded to O'Brian. The funeral director closed it, pushed the casket back in place, and led Longarm back upstairs.

In his office O'Brian slumped into his swivel chair. "Satisfied?"

"Not quite."

"Well?"

Longarm sat down in a chair by O'Brian's desk without being invited to and took out a cheroot. When he had the smoke going, he said, "How much are you getting out of this?"

O'Brian paled. "What in the hell are you drivin' at, deputy?"

"You mean you don't know?"

"If you're insinuatin' that I'd be a part of robbing these widows of their life's savings . . ."

"Yep, mister. That's just what I'm insinuating. You know what's going on around here, but downstairs I didn't see a single lock and no one was on guard. You're wide open—inviting them bastards to steal any corpse they want."

O'Brian pulled out a handkerchief from his back pocket and began mopping his brow. "If I don't cooperate, do you have any idea what these men would do?"

"Nothing. They'd just leave you alone. They don't want to create any kind of an uproar."

With a bitter laugh O'Brian took a desk-sized photograph out of his middle desk drawer, set it up on the desk, then turned it to face Longarm. It showed a young lady of sixteen or seventeen in a white dress and parasol smiling shyly at the camera. For the occasion she had unpinned her dark hair to allow the thick locks to coil down upon her shoulders. There was more than a vague resemblance to O'Brian. Longarm guessed she was his daughter. She was very pretty.

"My daughter, Marylou," O'Brian said heavily.

"She is very pretty."

"This man Thomaris—he's holding her. If I do not do as they say, I may never see her again."

"Where is he keeping her? In town here?"

"No. In Denver somewhere. Thomaris said as soon as they were ready to pull out, they'd give me her address and I could go get her. She'd be waiting for me."

"You believe them, do you?"

"Hell, Marshal, what choice do I have?"

"O'Brian, do you know where they're keeping the bodies?"

The funeral director looked with sudden fear at Longarm. "Hell, no," he said. "What makes you think they'd tell me a thing like that?"

Only he *did* know, Longarm realized, reading the man's eyes. He was just too terrified to tell him. And it would be useless to try to force it out of the man.

"How about MacGregor and Daniel?"

"They won't help you none, either. Daniel, they worked over pretty thoroughly. He showed me the bruises they left on him. All over, for Christ's sake. MacGregor's woman has been laid up now for close on to a year. She's completely bedridden. They threatened to set fire to his house and burn her alive in her bed. He's as terrified as we are."

"I don't wonder." Longarm looked at O'Brian closely. "You sure you won't tell me where they've got the bodies hid?"

"I've already told you more than I should have."

"Has Mrs. Devlin showed up yet with her ransom."

"No."

"What's the procedure?"

"Soon as I get the money, I'll send a boy over to the saloon. Kennedy or Thomaris will come for it."

"Where are they keeping the money?"

"How the hell should I know?"

"Must be quite a bundle by now."

"Look, Marshal, I can't tell you any more than I already have. Please, just get out of my office here before you foul up this whole operation. From what they've told me, Devlin's the last body they're going to kidnap. Soon as they get the money they're clearing out."

"Including Walt Kennedy?"

"Of course."

"What about his saloon?"

"He's already sold his share in it."

"Why are they clearing out now, they got such a good thing here?"

"Widow Sanders, raising such a stink—and then calling you in. And you been pressing them pretty hard. They figure it's time to leave."

"I'm glad to hear that."

"They don't like you none, mister. I'd be careful if I was you."

"That so?"

"That's what Thomaris told me."

"You believe him?"

"Why wouldn't I? He's the man in charge. And so far, he's done pretty well."

"Not for long."

"Give us a break, will you, Marshal? Don't mess things up. All any of us in this town want is for them devils to take their money and clear out of here."

"There's only one thing, O'Brian."

"What's that?"

"It's not their money."

O'Brian clamped his mouth shut. He couldn't argue that point, but Longarm could see that for him it really made no difference. All he could think of was his daughter held in a room somewhere in Denver, suffering God knows what indignities and outrages.

Longarm got up from the chair and headed for the door. O'Brian watched him balefully and said nothing as Longarm turned the knob, pulled the door open, and let himself out.

"Why, Deputy Long!" cried a familiar voice. "What a pleasure to see you again!"

On his way back to the hotel Longarm hauled up and turned to see Eileen Turnbill smiling up at him from under the wide brim of her black hat. Apparently, she had just stepped out of the woman's dress shop behind her.

Longarm touched his hatbrim to her. "Howdy, Eileen," he said agreeably. "Getting out, are you?"

"It's about time, wouldn't you say?"

"Guess so."

"I've been looking at some new dresses—for my coming-out party."

"I can hardly wait," said Longarm.

"You won't have to wait, Custis," she said archly. "Not if you don't want to."

"Thanks, Eileen. I appreciate the thought. But I'm pretty busy right now."

"I know all about that, Custis." She moved closer. "But . . . maybe I can help."

"What do you mean?"

"Isn't that why you came to visit me in the first place? You thought maybe I might know something about this terrible business."

"Yes, that's true."

"Well, then. I think perhaps it might be worth your while to come visit."

"When?"

"What's wrong with right now?"

"Nothing," he said warily. "I suppose."

She looked quickly around, her eyes alight with excitement. "Now, you must leave me here, and let me go on alone. If people saw me walking off down the street with such a handsome man, it would be a real scandal. Give me at least fifteen minutes."

"Sure. But I don't see as how you'll be kidding anyone. We've been standing right here talking in broad daylight in front of the whole town."

"Never you mind that, Custis. We must be discreet."

Longarm watched her hurry off, her hand steadying her wide hatbrim, aware that he had no business consorting with this particular widow, but aware also that perhaps—just perhaps—she might really have something of value to tell him.

The thing was, if she offered him nourishment, he would have to watch out for her flypaper soup.

Eileen's widow's weeds were nowhere in evidence when she opened the door to his knock and drew him into her entry hall. She was wearing a white, cloudlike negligee with pink ruffles that ran down her front and circled her wrists. Since the negligee was shockingly transparent, the ruffles left at least something to Longarm's imagination as she took his hat and helped him slip out of his frock coat. She hung his coat up in the hall closet, placed his hat on a shelf, then closed the closet door, took his hand, and began to lead him up the stairs to the bedroom. Longarm halted halfway up.

"What's the hurry, Eileen?"

"Why, whatever's wrong, Custis?" she asked, turning to face him. "You know your way up here, don't you?"

"What is this all about, Eileen? You said you had something to tell me—about the kidnappings. Remember?"

"I'll tell you afterward. Is that such a terrible prospect, Custis?"

"Eileen, I don't believe you have anything to tell me."

"Why, whatever do you mean?"

"You don't know anything more than you did before. You just wanted me to come over here."

"Yes." She smiled. "You're right. I cannot tell a lie. I wanted you and so I fibbed. Is that so bad?"

"It's deceitful."

"Yes, I'm simply terrible, aren't I? Now, do stop all this haggling and come up here with me, you great big wonderful man."

Longarm still hesitated. Something about this did not ring true. A careful, calculating part of her seemed to be peering out at him from under her thick brows. Her lush pouting lips trembled for a moment, as if she had experienced a chill, and her alabaster face looked paler than usual. From the moment he entered her house, she had been acting randy, too randy—as if she were dealing with a first-time hayseed on his way up to her crib.

"Custis? What's wrong? Why are you looking at me like that?"

"I'm just drinking you in, Eileen. That's very fetching negligee you're wearing."

She brightened. "It's from New Orleans. It's French."

"I never would have guessed."

She took his hand. "Let's not talk about what I'm wearing, Custis. I won't be wearing it for long."

Unwilling to pull his hand out of her grasp, he followed her up the stairs and into her bedroom. The covers of her bed were folded down neatly. There was a beaker of water and a decanter of brandy on a small table she had pulled over to the bed. She was ready for a party, and Longarm had been invited. Touched though he was by her eagerness and the thoroughness of her preparation, he still could not shake his nagging unease. She halted in front of the bed and spun about to face him.

"Shall I shock you?" she asked.

Before he could reply, she stepped out of her negligee and stood before him as naked as a Greek goddess and a whole hell of a lot more available. She stepped into his arms and, while she kissed him, helped him off with his cross-draw rig, peeled his vest over his shoulders, and began unbuttoning his shirt. By that time he had thrown caution to the winds. He knew what she was and that she was undoubtedly up to no good. But he also knew that he wanted her. He kicked off his boots and peeled out of his trousers and long johns.

Naked, locked in each other's embrace, they hit the bed, his lips devouring her breasts, her powerful legs scissoring his waist. He entered her with precious little foreplay, but she was moist and more than ready for him as she opened up her dark gates for his entry. Keening softly, her fingers running through his hair recklessly, she leaned back and sucked him in still deeper.

"What's that?" Longarm asked, rolling away from her and sitting up.

Pouting, Eileen sat up also. She was still flushed and eager. Her exploring tongue had caused Longarm to come awake again and he had been prowling over her, parting her thighs with his knees while she licked her lips in anticipation when he heard what he thought were footsteps on the stairs.

"I think I heard someone downstairs," Longarm told her.

He was reaching for his trousers when Marshal Boyd stepped into the bedroom, his sixgun cocked and ready.

"Not downstairs, Long," he said. "I'm already up here."

"Marshal Boyd!" Eileen cried, frantically pulling a bedsheet up over her breasts. "What are you doing in my house!"

"Now, don't tell me you're surprised."

"You said all you wanted was to get the deputy out of the way for a few hours. You said nothing about storming in here."

"No, but that was the plan, Miss Eileen," he said. "Afraid I wasn't exactly honest."

"You are a beastly . . . dishonest man, Marshal Boyd!"

"Yeah. Every time I think about it, I get to sobbing with remorse."

With Boyd's greedy eyes fastened on Eileen, Longarm reached down for his boot and then flung himself backward off the bed, landing on the floor behind it. Cursing, Boyd sent a wild flurry of rounds at Longarm, one of which slammed into the wall, the other shattering the bedroom window. Eileen screamed in terror. Longarm hugged the floor as he reached into his boot for the derringer. It wasn't there. He'd taken his left boot instead of his right. Longarm heard the bed squeak as Boyd stepped up onto it.

Longarm scooted under the bed. On the other side, still under the bed, he reached for his other boot and snatched the derringer out of it. He heard the bed squeak and the mattress sagged toward his head as Boyd jumped to the floor. Longarm poked his head out and saw Boyd staring down, the muzzle of his smoking sixgun yawning at him. Longarm ducked back a second before Boyd's gun thundered. The bullet whined off a bedspring and skittered like a crazed cockroach to the far wall.

"I'm hit, Boyd," Longarm called. "Hold up!"

Boyd stepped back and peered under the bed. The sight on Longarm's derringer found Boyd's face. Longarm squeezed the trigger. With a howl Boyd staggered back, turned, and bolted from the room. Longarm rolled out from under the bed, snatched his sixgun out of his rig, and reached the head of the stairs in time to see Boyd fling open the front door and run out. Longarm pounded down the stairs and was about to follow Boyd out the door when he realized he was stark naked.

He ducked into the living room, brushed aside the front window's drapes, and saw Boyd, holding his left shoulder as he pounded off down the street. In a moment he was out of sight. Longarm ran back up the stairs to get himself dressed.

"All clear," he told Eileen as he charged back into the bedroom. "You can come out from under them covers now."

When she didn't answer, he looked more closely at her ominously quiet form huddled under the blanket, then caught sight of the rapidly darkening bedsheet beneath her.

"Eileen!" he called, rushing to her side.

Chapter 9

Whining like a stuck pig, Boyd flung himself up the wooden stairs leading from the alley to Walt Kennedy's apartment. When he found the door on the landing locked, he pounded on it with his fist until he brought an angry Walt Kennedy to the door.

"Who the hell is it?" Walt demanded through it.

"It's me, for Christ's sake," moaned Boyd. "Open the door! I'm hurt bad!"

The door swung open and Walt grabbed Boyd's gunbelt and drew him quickly into the kitchen, slammed the door, and whirled to look the town marshal over, his eyes filled with a weary contempt.

"What about Long?" he demanded.

"I winged him maybe. But the bastard got me in my left shoulder." Boyd's face twisted in self-pity. "Jesus, it hurts, Walt. You better get the doc up here!"

"You know better than that, Boyd. He's in the bag by now, his boots filled with his own piss."

"I don't care! Get him! Drunk or sober, he's the only man who can get this slug out of me."

"You say you winged Long? You sure of that?"

"He cried out when I hit him. And when I bent over to see, he blasted me. Sure, he's hurt, but I don't know how bad."

"I think you're a liar—and you've got a wide stripe of mustard down your back. And right now you're bleeding all over my floor. Sit down over there at the table. I'll get some towels for you to hold against your shoulder to stop all that bleeding—and then I'll go for the doc. Meanwhile, asshole, do what you can to shut up."

"Hey, Walt," Boyd whined. "What is all this? Ain't we in this together?"

"Yeah—and right now that's what's making me sick to my stomach. One more thing. When I go for the doc, I don't want you sneakin' in to raid my liquor cabinet. You got that?"

"Sure. Sure," Boyd said bitterly.

"Good," Walt snapped.

He turned and left the kitchen to get the towels.

Longarm shouldered through the Last Chance's batwings and saw Walt Kennedy at a table in the rear bent over the slumping Dante. He was shaking his shoulder to wake him. There was no doubt in Longarm's mind why Kennedy was attempting to arouse the soused doc—so he could patch up the wounded town marshal.

Without pause, Longarm pushed through the crowded saloon. When he reached the doc's table, Dante, foul with stale whiskey fumes, had already managed to lift his head and was staring blearily at Kennedy. At the sight of Longarm stopping beside Kennedy, he blinked and brightened slightly. He was trying hard to regain his senses, but was obviously in desperate need of the hair of the dog.

"What the hell do you want, Long?" Kennedy demanded.

"I want the doc."

"What the hell for?"

"Never mind that, get him a bottle of your rotgut and hurry it up."

"You can't tell me what—"

With the heel of his right palm, Longarm hit Kennedy on the left shoulder, spinning him around, then booted him halfway to the bar. Just able to maintain his balance, Kennedy staggered the remaining few feet to it, snatched a nearly full bottle from an amazed patron, and returned with it to the doc's table.

Longarm took the bottle from him and thrust it into the doc's trembling hands. Like a baby reaching blindly for the teat, Dante pulled the bottle toward him, closed his lips around its neck, and lifted it nearly vertical as he poured the medicine down his gullet.

"I won't forget this," snarled Kennedy.

Longarm looked at him. "I sincerely hope not. Where's Boyd?"

"How the hell would I know that?"

"He's upstairs, ain't he?"

"You're loco."

"You're the one that's crazy if you think you can hide that son of a bitch from me. He's shot up Eileen Turnbill pretty bad. If the doc can't save her, he's a murderer—and I'm a witness. You tell that son of a bitch I'm coming after him."

"Boyd? He shot Eileen Turnbill?"

"You heard me."

"I didn't know nothin' about that. I thought . . ."

"Yeah. You thought it was me he'd gone after. Well, it was, but he made a botch of it."

Obviously stunned by this news, Kennedy took a step back, his face pale. "I swear, Long, I had nothin' to do with this. Nothin'."

"You're a liar, Kennedy," Longarm told him bluntly, "and not even a good one."

"Hey, you got no cause to—"

"Shut up and listen. Soon's I get the doc to look at Eileen Turnbill, I'm coming back for that son of a bitch I winged. If you and that New Yorker give me any trouble, I'll maybe have to take you both to perdition with him."

Longarm turned his back on Kennedy and hauled the doc to his feet. Grabbing the bottle, the doc allowed himself to be pushed through the growing crowd of gaping patrons and out the door. The sunlight almost blinded him; he spun his face away as if someone had whipped it.

"You all right, doc?" Longarm asked, grabbing his upper arm.

"Yeah," the man mumbled. "That sun sure is bright."

"Let's go."

"Custis!"

Longarm turned to see Jean Langly. He held up and waited for her to reach them.

Breathless, she asked, "Why, Custis, I thought you were up in your room sleeping!"

"Not likely."

"Whatever is going on?"

"The doc here is going to need some help. Eileen Turnbill has been shot up pretty bad."

"Shot up?"

"It's a long story. I'll fill you in later, but right now you can be mighty useful, I'm thinking."

"Me?"

"The doc's going to need help."

At the mention of his name, the doc swayed and almost lost the bottle in his hand. Longarm grabbed the whiskey and steadied the man. Dante blinked and shook his head to clear it.

"I'm all right," he mumbled. "Just don't lose that bottle."

"Come on," Longarm said urgently. "We can't waste any time."

The three hurried on down the street, a threesome that caught many an eye and set scores of tongues to wagging. And if that were not enough, there soon came the account of how Longarm had just handled Walt Kennedy in his own saloon. The news spread through town with the speed of a prairie fire.

• • •

Walt Kennedy was almost beside himself with rage. He didn't know if it was shame or anger that had just been etched on his soul; it was probably a mixture of both, but when he burst into the kitchen and saw Boyd resting his head facedown on the kitchen table, his blood trickling off the wooden chair onto the floor, and realized the son of a bitch had made no effort to use the towels he had brought him to staunch the flow of blood, he had difficulty keeping himself from finishing him off with a single well-placed bullet.

He grabbed the man by the hair and flung his head back. With a startled yelp Boyd's eyes flew open.

"Jesus, Walt, what's the matter with you?"

"What's the matter with *you,* you stupid son of a bitch! Why didn't you tell me what you done?"

"What do you mean?" Boyd bleated, pulling back from Walt's fury. "I already told you."

"You didn't tell me shit. What about that dame? Eileen Turnbill."

"What's she got to do with anything?"

"You shot her up, you stupid bastard. Long was downstairs. He just grabbed the doc. He's on the way over to her house with him now."

"Oh, my God, did I shoot her?"

"You sure as hell didn't shoot Long."

"It was a mistake, Walt, so help me."

"I know it was a mistake, you silly bastard. But I'm gettin' out of this right now. That U.S. marshal said he was coming back for you and warned me and Thomaris to stay out of it. And that's just what I'm going to do."

"What do you mean?" Boyd cried, close to panic.

"I mean I'm kicking you out of here. You got one chance the way I see it, mister. Get on a horse and ride—and don't look back."

"But . . . my money!"

"I'll get your share. You can have it. As soon as Thomaris gets that money waitin' at O'Brian's we're pullin' out, too."

"Let me stay here, Walt," Boyd pleaded. "I'm bleedin' like a stuck pig."

"And you're whinin' like one, too. I'll get your share."

"Please, Walt."

Walt ignored his plea and left the kitchen. When he returned a few minutes later, Boyd had taken out his sixgun and laid it on the table, his hand closed firmly about the grips, his finger coiled about the trigger. When Walt saw what Boyd intended, he dropped the satchel he was carrying, ducked low, and rushed him. The gun in Boyd's hand thundered. The round missed Walt and crashed into the wall behind him. Crunching into Boyd with vicious force, Walt sent him toppling back off his chair. As Boyd hit the floor he uttered a muffled cry and dropped his weapon. Walt kicked it and sent it spinning into a corner, then hauled Boyd upright.

"You tried to kill me," Walt said meanly.

"Why not, you bastard? You're as good as killing me, sending me out of here with this bullet in my shoulder."

Walt grinned meanly at him. "For a dying man, you sure as hell got a lot of bleat left in you."

He thrust the satchel of money into Boyd's right hand, then spun him around and marched him to the door, one hand twisting his right arm up behind him. As he slammed into the door Boyd twisted his head around to look at Walt.

"My gun!" he cried. "What about my gun? You can't send me out of here without no weapon!"

Walt picked Boyd's sixgun off the floor, broke it open, and dropped the remaining cartridges into his palm, then tucked the empty gun into Boyd's holster. Then he pulled open the door and pushed him out onto the landing; a moment later, as Boyd cried out in dismay, he flung him down the wooden steps. Boyd hit the alley floor hard, sprawling facedown. When he got up, he glanced wildly up at Walt, then staggered off down the alley, cutting down a side street leading to Main Street a moment later.

Good, thought Walt. He'd get his horse from the livery and ride out. Or maybe he'd be fool enough to go after Long. Walt closed the door and walked back through the kitchen, ignoring the huge bloodstain under the chair.

He was still shaking somewhat from the action of a few moments before, and his rage at how Long had treated him downstairs in the Last Chance had faded somewhat. He allowed as how he was so upset he couldn't function. But with just him and Thomaris left, that meant bigger splits for both of them. When Boyd got the chance to look into that satchel, he'd be one surprised son of a bitch. But why give money to a dead man?

Walt had seen this coming and had already hired a closed coach to take him and Thomaris to Denver. When Thomaris returned from O'Brian's with the money, they'd be on their way.

The doc had sobered—even retired his whiskey bottle to the top of the dresser—when he saw how badly Eillen Turnbill had been wounded. She had taken two rounds, one in the thigh, the other just below her breast on the left side. In addition she had obviously lost a considerable amount of blood.

Taking advantage of the fact that she was unconscious, the doc dug out the slug in her thigh, but when he probed for the slug that had entered her left side, he had to give it up, then dress both wounds. In this task Jean's help was greatly appreciated, since by now Dante's hands were trembling as if he had the ague.

Dante stepped back finally from the bed, stroking his ragged Vandyke beard, regarding his patient with unhappy eyes.

"How bad is she?" Longarm asked.

"I got to get that second bullet out," the doc told Longarm. "But I don't know where it's gone. It could be in there anywhere. Might have ranged clear up to her neck for all I know."

"Then she's in a bad way."

He nodded glumly. "And she's lost a lot of blood, maybe too much."

"Isn't there anything we can do?" Jean asked.

"Keep her quiet is all I can think," the doc said.

"Maybe with plenty of bed rest, she'll pull through."

"With that bullet in her?"

"I said, maybe."

He reached for the bottle on the dresser and took a healthy belt. It seemed to steady him.

Longarm looked down at Eileen. She was coming around. He moved closer as she opened her eyes and peered up at him, fear clouding her eyes.

"How do you feel?" Longarm asked.

"I hurt," she whispered. "Inside. I'm on fire."

The doc hurried over. "Where, exactly."

"My lungs. I can't hardly breathe, doc."

Dante looked around at Longarm, his drawn face revealing the hopelessness he felt. Then he beckoned Longarm away from the bed. As Longarm backed off, the Doc leaned over Eileen and pressed slowly down on her left breast. He got no real response until he tried her right breast. Choking, Eileen twisted convulsively under the pressure. The doc pulled quickly back.

As Jean hurried over to comfort Eileen the doc guided Longarm back to the dresser and, turning his back on the bed, looked with little hope at Longarm. "The slug's in her right lung," he said. "Nothing I can do."

"Then Boyd's a murderer."

"Not right now, but he soon will be." Dante squinted at Longarm. "You mind tellin' me what you was doing up here in the first place?"

Longarm had difficulty keeping his angry response down. "What in the hell do you think I was doing?"

Dante raised a hand and stepped back. "Just askin'."

Longarm left the doc and returned to the bed. Framed in her pile of dark, chestnut hair, Eileen's alabaster cheeks had even less color than usual and her richly dark eyes showed only fear now. She reached up and took his sleeve and drew him down.

"Am I going to die, Custis?"

"We don't have to talk about that now."

"Yes, we do!" she said desperately.

"Why?"

"Because I'm going to hell! I can feel the fires of damnation, Custis!"

"That's a foolish thing to say, Eileen."

"No, it ain't. Not for what I done!"

"Shh! Don't think about it."

"Alfred . . . he'll be waitin' for me, Custis. Him and those awful, accusing eyes. He knew what I done at the last. He told me."

"There's nothing I can say, Eileen."

"Pray for me!"

"All right."

She closed her eyes and let her head sink back into the pillow. Longarm waited for her to open her eyes again. But she lay very still. And when he saw how quiet her breasts were, he glanced quickly, nervously over at the doc. He came fast and bent over her, taking up her slender wrist in his trembling hands. It took only a moment. He looked at Longarm and shook his head. As he drew the sheet up over her head Jean gasped and turned her head, burying her face in her hands.

Longarm went over and put a comforting arm on her shoulder.

"Let's go downstairs. There's nothing more you can do here."

Jean nodded and let him lead her down the stairs to the front room. They sat on the sofa in its cool darkness. Eileen had not pulled back the satin drapes.

"What did she mean?" Jean asked.

"That business about hellfire?"

Swearing her to silence, Longarm told her. When he finished, Jean shuddered.

"My God," she whispered. "What a terrible thing to carry to the grave with you."

"Amen to that."

"And you were up here with her—when Boyd came after you."

Longarm nodded glumly. "He'd put her up to it—though he didn't tell her exactly what he intended."

"Which was to murder you while you were in bed with her."

"Not very pretty, I admit."

She looked at him closely and was about to say something. Longarm had a pretty good idea what was on her mind. It had to with him being able to take on this widow while begging off comforting her. But she had the good sense to bite her tongue and say nothing about it. For that he was grateful. This was sure as hell not the time for that kind of discussion.

"What are you going to do?" she asked.

"Go back to the Last Chance. Kennedy's got Boyd holed up there. I want him."

"You sure he's still there?"

"I wounded him. He's likely in no shape to travel."

"Custis, I think this kidnapping business is all winding down."

"What do you mean?"

"Kennedy's rented a closed carriage and a strong team. He's going to Denver, I hear. Today."

Longarm nodded. "Yeah. With the loot. Soon's he gets the money waiting for him at O'Brian's."

"You've got to stop them."

"I intend to."

The doc came down the stairs and looked over at them. He was holding the whiskey bottle by its neck, but he looked coldly, bleakly sober. He entered the front room and slumped into an easy chair still draped in black.

"You going to pray for Eileen?" he asked Longarm.

"I am."

"Then pray for me. I knew what she done to that asshole husband of hers—and I covered for her. I told everyone it was a heart attack."

Longarm said nothing as the doc glared bleakly at him.

"So when you pray, pray for me, too."

"I'll do that, doc."

Dante lifted the bottle to his mouth and tipped his head back, hoping it appeared, for a quick oblivion. Longarm got to his feet.

"I got to be going, doc."

"Go ahead. Both of you. I'll tell the funeral home."

Longarm escorted Jean from the room and together they walked back to Main Street. He told her he was going into the saloon to bring out Boyd and suggested she wait for him in her hotel room. She started to argue when Walt Kennedy pushed through his batwings and came to halt on the saloon porch. He was hefting a rifle.

"You comin' in here, Long?"

"Yes," Longarm told him, starting up the steps. "I told you I'd be back for Boyd. There's a dead woman he's got to pay for."

"He's gone. I kicked him the hell out. You won't find him here."

Longarm halted on the third step, realizing this was something he should have counted on. There was no honor among thieves—or grave robbers, either, it seemed.

"That's right, Marshal!" a voice called from across the street.

Longarm turned to see who had spoken and was mildly astonished to see how quickly the street in front of the Last Chance was filling up with excited spectators. Beyond the growing crowd, the hostler was standing in front of the livery beside his stable boy; it was he who had spoken up.

"You seen him go?" Longarm called.

"Cleared out a good half hour ago, I'd say. He was riding his big blue and bleedin' like a stuck pig."

"I saw him ride out, too," someone in the crowd told Longarm.

Others quickly chimed in. Longarm turned back around to look up at the gun-toting gambler. "You know the man. Where'd he be headin'?"

"Beats the shit out of me, Long. But don't worry. He won't get far, not with your bullet in him."

"I'll be back, Kennedy," Longarm said quietly. "When I do, I don't think you should be hefting a rifle. It wouldn't be smart."

Longarm turned and descended the steps. He spoke quietly to Jean, asking her to keep an eye on Kennedy and Thomaris while he went after Boyd. He promised he wouldn't be long, then pushed through the crowd toward the livery stable.

Chapter 10

When Thomaris walked into O'Brian's office, he found Golden's three undertakers waiting for him. O'Brian was sitting behind his desk, a shoe box filled with bank notes in front of him—a sawed-off shotgun resting on the desk beside it. O'Brian's finger was coiled about the trigger.

"Both barrels are loaded," Silas MacGregor told Thomaris, his jaw solid with resolve.

"That's right," seconded Jim Daniel.

"Well, well, well," said Thomaris softly. He adjusted the toothpick in his mouth. "The worms have turned."

"That they have," said Silas.

Thomaris looked the tall, angular Scotsman over

shrewdly. Silas was obviously their spokesman. He had to have been the one who had managed finally to stiffen the backbones of these other two.

"Silas," he said, "you don't think I got the time yet to burn you out?"

"That time has passed," Silas said.

"You think so, do you?"

"We know so," said O'Brian. "We been doing some counting ourselves."

"That so?"

"Since that U.S. deputy marshal rode in, your gang has been whittled down to bite size," Jim Daniel said, his gimlet eyes peering triumphantly through his spectacles at Thomaris.

"Dick Pratt's gone," continued O'Brian. "The widow Sanders took care of him. Then there's Boyd's deputies, Tucker and Slim. We figure the deputy marshal finished them off. And maybe you ain't heard yet about Boyd. He murdered Eileen Turnbill and the deputy marshal's wounded him bad. He's holed up in the livery right now, but it wouldn't surprise any of us to see him light out anytime now."

"So that means it's just you and Kennedy now," said Silas.

Grinning at the three desperate undertakers, Thomaris flicked away his toothpick. "And you three figure you're a match for me and Walt, that it?"

He could hardly believe how easy these three bumpkins were making it for him. And now with Boyd out of it, there was one less to share their take with. Yes, sir, things were working out nicely.

"All right," Thomaris said lightly. "You three outlaws got me cold turkey. So what are you after?"

"This here two thousand," Silas replied promptly.

"And a share of all that other money you've been hauling in," said Jim Daniel, pushing his spectacles back onto his nose.

Daniel was all bright-eyed and bushy-tailed, eager for his share of this ill-gotten gain. Standing out on his forehead, though, were tiny, gleaming beads of perspiration. Hell, if Thomaris was any judge, these three were shitting in their pants right now, even though they were doing their best to hide it.

"Just how much of a share do you want?" Thomaris asked teasingly. "Would half of what we pulled in be enough?"

"We are not greedy men," Silas said.

"That so?"

"Three thousand—for each of us."

"You going to count what's in this shoe box?"

"Yes," Silas said.

"Which means you'll settle for seven thousand from what we've already taken."

"Yes."

Thomaris laughed in their faces. "Hell's fire, gents! That ain't much! Why not take all of it? If Walt and I are in such bad shape and all. Why, it would be like taking licorice from a baby."

The three men shifted nervously. They couldn't understand why he was taking it the way he was, obviously. Thomaris should have been shaking in his boots, especially with a loaded shotgun aimed at his gut.

"Don't take us lightly," Silas warned Thomaris.

"And if I don't, you say O'Brian here will blast me in two with his shotgun. That it?"

"You put it crudely," said Silas. "But you're right. So you better cooperate."

"You think so, do you?"

"Don't forget. We have the law on our side," Daniel reminded him.

"You know what?" said Thomaris. "You ain't thought this through. You shoot me, all you'll get is what's in this shoe box. Two thousand."

"We know where to get the rest," said Silas.

"Oh, sure," Thomaris said, laughing. "Just run down to the Last Chance, blast Kennedy, then take the money—and not a soul in Golden will know what you done."

"Maybe we'll just take what's in this shoebox," said Silas.

"Sure. If I let you have it," Thomaris reminded him.

O'Brian cleared his throat. "All right, all right. I'm sick of all this talk, fellows. I don't care about the money. Thomaris can have my share. I got a deal to make with him."

"Let's hear it," said Thomaris.

"You know what I want. You promised to tell me where you're keeping my daughter."

"Ah, yes, the lovely Marylou. You want her back, do you?"

Tight-lipped, O'Brian nodded.

"But if I tell you, it wouldn't be right. You aren't keeping your part of the bargain, remember? You're throwing in with these two outlaws."

"I told you. You can have my share for Marylou's return."

"And you think that's fair, do you?"

"Goddammit, Thomaris! Where you holding her?"

"Clancy Street in Denver," Thomaris told him. "Second floor. Apartment fourteen. She's waiting there now—but not for me to bring her back to this dust hole in the middle of nowhere, O'Brian. She's waitin' for me, and this money I'm bringin' her!"

"You lie!"

"You're a fool, O'Brian. Did you really think I took Marylou from this turd of a town against her will?"

"I don't believe you!"

"Then don't. Just don't expect Marylou back. Not of her own free will, anyway. Do you really think she wants to spend the best years of her life in a funeral home, a place filled with the stench of death?"

Tears of rage filled O'Brian's eyes. He tried to speak, but couldn't. It was clear he had suspected all along the truth behind his daughter's disappearance, but he had stubbornly fought against facing it. His two companions, embarrassed, looked away and said nothing. They, too, had known why Marylou had vanished from her father's home.

"All right then, you bastard," said O'Brian, his voice nasty. "No deal. This here money is ours—all of it. And we want the other seven thousand. We'll keep you here as our prisoner and send a message to Kennedy. Either he comes through with the money, or you're a dead man."

"You crazy? Can you think of anything Walt would want more than me out of the way? He'll just take my share and light out."

The undeniable truth of this stunned the three men.

Jim Daniel looked at Silas. "We never thought of that."

"It don't matter," said O'Brian grimly. "We'll kill this son of a bitch right here and now and take the two thousand. It's better than nothing."

Thomaris looked calmly at O'Brian. "You sure you can kill a man in cold blood?"

"No problem," said O'Brian. "I know how to use this shotgun."

"I'm sure you do. But I don't think you will."

"Try me," said O'Brian.

"Sure," said Thomaris.

As he spoke he ducked low and rammed the desk into O'Brian. Still in his chair, O'Brian slammed back against the wall, his fingers tightening on the shotgun's trigger. There was no detonation, however. Thomaris snatched the shotgun out of the dismayed O'Brian's grasp. All the while it had been resting on the desktop, Thomaris had known its safety was still on. Turning the shotgun around, Thomaris released the catch and leveled it at the three terrified undertakers.

"I always love it when amateurs try to take matters into their own hands," he said. He glanced at O'Brian. "Put the cover on that shoe box and drop it into the top drawer."

A chastened O'Brian pushed the desk forward to give himself room. Then he pulled open the drawer, dropped the shoe box into it, and slammed the drawer shut.

"Now, gents," Thomaris said, stepping back, "we're going downstairs to the vault. Don't make any sudden moves. You should know by now you're just puppy dogs—you ain't up to handling real wolves." He grinned and waggled the shotgun's barrel at them. "Come on now, get a move on."

With O'Brian in the lead, the three undertakers filed out of his office and headed down a narrow hallway to the basement door. Through it—O'Brian still in the lead—they filed, moving down a flight of steps to a narrow passageway lit by a pair of dim, smoking kerosene lamps hanging on nails attached to the wall. Obviously familiar with the place, Thomaris directed the three men past the embalming room and to the vault. The three men halted.

"Open the doors," Thomaris told O'Brian.

O'Brian unlocked the wide doors and led them into the vault. Only a single lamp was glowing inside it, and that feebly, its chimney black with soot. Thomaris told O'Brian and the other two to light the lamps hanging from the walls above the caskets.

Once they had done so, the full extent of the banks of waiting caskets was visible, resplendent in their silver and gold trimmings and clasps, their rich polished mahogany and oak gleaming darkly. They presented a brilliant, if somber, display—and once again Thomaris was struck by the utter waste of spending so much time, effort, and money on these final resting places for the dead. Was he the only one who realized that the corpses contained in these spectacular coffins were but empty hulls—like those cicada husks he used to find under oak trees on hot summer mornings when he was a boy. The living souls had long since fled their loathsome encumbrance, their loathsome flesh.

And yet, astonishingly enough, after he had hid them so cleverly, there was nothing these fool widows would not pay to have these dried-out, blackened husks returned to them. What fools! Thus did they dispose of the wealth their departed husbands had labored to leave them. He chuckled out loud at the thought. At the sound the three puzzled undertakers drew back. They were watching him with furtive, narrowed eyes. The thought occurred to Thomaris that perhaps they were considering whether or not to rush him and wrest the shotgun from his grasp.

"Go ahead!" he taunted them suddenly, holding the shotgun out to them. "Take it! Here's your big chance! Free yourselves and take the money waiting upstairs!"

Thoroughly disconcerted by this offer, the three men cringed back from him still further. No doubt about it. They thought he was as mad as a hatter.

With a short, contemptuous burst of laughter, he flung the shotgun down at their feet. They froze at sight of it, and before they could make a move toward it, Thomaris drew his .38-caliber Smith & Wesson from his shoulder rig, then kicked the shotgun out of his way and moved menacingly closer to them, his eyes on Silas, the one he considered the toughest of the three.

"Okay, Silas. No more games. Time's running out. Go find an empty casket."

"A casket?"

"You heard me. One of the more expensive."

"What . . . what for?"

"You need a rest."

"A rest? In a coffin? You're mad!"

"Yeah. Maybe so." Thomaris cocked his revolver. "Go ahead. Do like I say."

Like someone walking in his sleep, Silas moved a few feet down the row of caskets and stopped at one very large one, lifted the lid, and peered nervously into its gleaming, silky interior. Thomaris recognized it as one of those he had already redesigned—which sure made it all the more appropriate, now that he thought of it.

"Go on. Get into it," he told Silas.

"You can't mean this," Silas said, incredulous.

Thomaris took a step closer to the undertaker. "Jesus. Didn't you hear me, old man? I said get in there and lie down."

When Silas saw the furious gleam in Thomaris's eyes, all fight drained out of him and he pulled the casket's platform out, opened the lid all the way, and stepped carefully into the casket. As soon as he was prone on his back, his long head resting on a satin pillow, Thomaris moved quickly forward and slapped the lid down.

Then he turned to the others. "Let's go, you two, find an empty casket and get in."

"But, my God, man. We'll smother!" protested O'Brian.

"No, you won't." Thomaris grinned maliciously. "I'll leave a hole for you to breathe through. Hurry up!"

"But why," wailed Daniel.

Thomaris saw the two of them were about ready to shit in their pants. Already they were shaking like trees in the wind.

"Hey," he said. "No need to get nervous. All I want is you three out of the way until Walt and I show our heels to this town."

This explanation—silly as it was—seemed to steady the two men. Each one chose a casket and got in carefully, leaning their heads back with great care, obviously fearful they might dirty the coffins' virgin interiors. O'Brian seemed especially careful. These caskets were his merchandise, after all, and it would seriously depress his future profits if they were anything less than immaculate.

When it came time for the two men to pull the lids down over their upturned faces, they hesitated. They seemed frozen in terror at the thought. Thomaris strode forward impatiently and slammed both lids down, their velvet-lined edges thumping together snugly. Thomaris promptly snapped the lid clasps on all three caskets, locking them in.

At once a storm of muffled cries arose from the three caskets. All three were shouting the same thing. With the lids locked firmly, they could not breathe! They would suffocate! Silas's cries were the most frantic by far. He had been in his casket the longest and was probably already having the most difficulty breathing. Thomaris imagined his face—and perhaps his entire splinter of a body as well—bathed in cold sweat.

Leaning close to the casket containing Silas, Thomaris called out loudly, "Hey, no need to fuss, Silas. Here's a hole to let in some air."

He rested the muzzle of his revolver on top of the casket's lid and, pointing straight down, fired. The round made a small, neat hole and silenced Silas immediately. Thomaris ventilated the other two caskets in the same fashion.

He was about to holster his weapon when he heard someone running down the cellar stairs, then approaching the vault. He turned to face whoever it was. In a moment, through the vault's open doors, swept the small, compact figure of O'Brian's apprentice. As always, the man smelled of embalming fluid and rotting entrails. Without bothering to explain a thing to this walking carrion, Thomaris lifted his revolver and fired point-blank into the man's chest. The apprentice dropped, lifeless, at Thomaris's feet. Thomaris dragged him into a dark corner behind a casket, then holstered his weapon and hurried from the vault, closing the doors behind him.

Then he hurried up the cellar steps, chuckling.

Walt was probably pissing in his pants by this time as he waited for him to collect this last haul.

Still heading southwest after the fleeing town marshal, Longarm pulled up and dismounted beside a shallow stream, then led his horse into the water, making sure the mount did not abuse the privilege and drink too much. He filled his canteen, drank deep from it, then topped it off and led the horse out of the water. Boyd's tracks were visible in the sand approaching the stream. They were so recent no moisture had yet crept into the hoofprints. But Boyd's closeness was no surprise to Longarm. He had had the man in sight now for nearly an hour.

He swung back aboard his mount and urged it on across the stream.

There were only two hours of sunlight left when the flat prairie lifted into rolling dunes cut by sand and clay gulches. Here and there a lone pine tree stood as an advance sentinel to the hills before him, which lay black and bulky and high along the western horizon.

Ahead of him in the distance, Boyd's mounted figure topped a crest, then vanished. Boyd had not looked back, but he had to know Longarm was on his trail. What amazed Longarm was the distance the wounded Boyd had ridden so far. But he couldn't keep it up. Before long he would have to dismount and hole up.

Longarm kept doggedly on, waiting—and hoping—for the worm to turn.

High in the bench lands, the trail cut through a sheer-walled canyon, one side of it a cliff reaching straight up, gray and weathered, showing as many cracks and fissures as an old plaster ceiling. Beyond the canyon, the dark bulk of the Rockies rose into the sky, closer now, formidable, great ramparts that seemed flung up before him as a warning.

He caught the glint of a rifle barrel high in the rocks ahead of him.

Good.

Boyd had finally come to roost.

Longarm pushed his horse to a sudden hard gallop, waiting for the shot he knew must come—gambling that when it did, it would go wild. After all, Boyd was severely wounded and, according to the hostler in Golden, bleeding like a stuck pig.

Longarm had just about concluded that Boyd had given up the idea of ambush when a rifle's crack sent a flurry of echoes rattling off the steep rock walls about him. At the same time a bullet whined uncomfortably close and ricocheted off a boulder. Longarm yanked his Winchester from its scabbard and flung himself from his saddle, slapped his horse's rump to send it farther down the canyon, then found cover in the boulders under the canyon's rim.

Boyd's shot had not been a poor one. Perhaps the son of a bitch was not as badly wounded as he had led everyone to believe.

Longarm poked his head out from behind the boulder and gazed up at the rocks on the other side of the canyon, looking for another gleam of sunlight on metal. He caught it just as another shot sent echoes crackling around him. The ricocheting bullet was undeniably closer this time. Boyd had Longarm pretty well locked in. But Longarm remembered the vantage point from which that last glint had come and was confident he could outflank it—if he could keep from getting his ass shot off when he broke out.

Keeping his ass down, he ducked out of cover and headed at a pounding run for the canyon's far wall. Boyd pocked the ground with slugs, but always a few feet behind him, until Longarm ducked into a light stand of pine, kept going through them, then angled up the rock-strewn slope behind them. He found a game trail and scrambled up it, keeping his long frame low, moving with the speed of a big cat. From above came a few prayerful, desultory shots as Boyd tried to find him. A few rounds came close, but not close enough to bother Longarm. It was clear Boyd had no idea where Longarm was now and was shooting simply to keep up his courage.

Longarm reached the crest and ran along it about twenty yards, then scrambled from there to a shale-littered trail, which he followed into a pile of rimrocks. He kept going until he judged himself to be above the spot where Boyd had forted up. He droppped to the back of a flat rock ledge and inched his way out onto it until he could see Boyd, crouched behind a boulder less than a hundred feet below, his horse cropping the grass in the shade of some rocks a few feet back. Boyd's rifle rested on a shelf of rock in front of him. He had an unobstructed view of the canyon floor below him and most of the trail Longarm had used to reach the rim. His head was craned far out as he searched for some sign of Longarm.

Pulling back suddenly, Boyd reached into his hip pocket and pulled out a fifth of whiskey. He tipped it up, gulped greedily, then stuck the bottle back into his pocket. He was living on rotgut, it appeared, and from the look of him, he was bleeding still and as drunk as a reservation Indian. Longarm no longer felt so much pride in outflanking the bastard.

"Boyd!" he called. "Drop your rifle!"

Boyd whirled, caught sight of Longarm's face, and fired up at him. Longarm ducked back as the slug whined off the rock face beneath him. When he looked down again, Boyd was scrambling back out of range, pulling his horse after him. Longarm sighted quickly and fired. The bullet seared the horse's flank like a brand. The animal reared wildly, pulling the reins from Boyd's grasp. Whinnying shrilly, the horse bolted ahead of him. Boyd turned, lifted his rifle, and fired another futile shot up at Longarm.

Longarm pushed himself back off the boulder, regained the canyon ridge, and retracing his previous route, dropped back down onto the game trail. He charged down it at full speed and was just in time to catch the clink of hooves against stone. He ducked aside just as Boyd's horse charged out of a narrow gully about ten feet above him and bolted past, nostrils flared, eyes wild. Longarm crouched below the gully, his rifle at the ready. Then came the chink of Boyd's spurs, and a moment later he charged into view.

"Drop that rifle, Boyd!" Longarm told him.

But the man did not have that much sense. Eyes wild, desperate, he flung up his rifle with his right hand and fired at Longarm. Ducking, Longarm fired twice, levering swiftly. Dust puffed as neat holes appeared in Boyd's vest, the slugs hurling him violently backward onto the rocky trail.

Longarm climbed up beside him. The stench of cheap rotgut hung heavy in the air. Longarm realized Boyd must have shattered the fifth he carried in his hip pocket when he went down. He bent close. The man's eyes were frozen open in death.

Longarm went looking for Boyd's horse.

His knees digging into the hard ground, Thomaris unrolled his blanket onto his slicker. Kennedy walked over and stood between him and the campfire to watch him. Thomaris got to his feet, picked up his saddle, and dropped it carefully down onto his blanket.

"That saddle makes a pretty hard pillow, John," Kennedy remarked, grinning. "You sure you can handle it?"

Thomaris adjusted the toothpick in the corner of his mouth. "I'm no tenderfoot, if that's what you mean."

"That's what I mean."

"Well, maybe you're right. I ain't anxious to sleep out here under a cold sky. You sure we couldn't've rode on into Denver, Walt? Seems silly to camp out here if we don't have to."

"I'd dead, John. Done in. You must be, too. We need this chance to rest up. Denver's a good five-hour ride away."

"So you say. But it sure would be stupid to let that crazy deputy marshal catch up to us out here."

"Forget that bastard. I told you. He ain't after us. He's still after Boyd—and Boyd'll give him hell when the two meet. We don't have to worry about him."

"So you say."

"That's right," Kennedy snapped. "So I say."

Without further comment, Thomaris took off his derby hat and dropped it beside the saddle. Kennedy turned and walked over to his own blanket. Thomaris tugged off his boots, dropped to the blanket and pulled it up around his shoulder, and tried to find a comfortable spot on the saddle to rest his cheek.

Then he closed his eyes.

But he did not sleep.

A half hour later Walt Kennedy's shadow once more came between Thomaris and the campfire—which had died down considerably by this time and was visible only as a dim glow. Watching from under his lowered lids, Thomaris caught the menacing gleam of Kennedy's sixgun as he lifted it slowly out of his holster and leveled it on Thomaris's sleeping form. He waited for Kennedy to cock the sixgun before he lifted his own, already-cocked .38 from under his blanket and sent two quick rounds into Kennedy's gut.

The man screamed and dropped his gun. Grabbing at his bloody, pulsing entrails, he staggered back and down, his body hitting the ground with what for Thomaris was a satisfying crunch. Thomaris flung aside his blanket and walked over to look down at the writhing gambler. Kennedy was holding on to his leaking entrails, his eyes wide with pain and terror. In the dim moonlight they reminded Thomaris of two fogged-over snake eyes.

"Holy shit, John!" Kennedy bleated. "What'd you do that for?"

"Why, you silly bastard," Thomaris said, grinning. "You telling me you don't know?"

Thomaris cocked his revolver, aimed at Kennedy's face, and fired. Then he cocked and fired again. Kennedy's pale face vanished into something large and bloody. Thomaris returned to his blanket and, kneeling on the ground, carefully rolled it up along with his slicker. Then he saddled his horse, mounted up, and with Kennedy's two bulging carpetbags hanging from his saddle horn, booted his horse toward Denver.

It was after midnight when Longarm rode into Golden, Boyd's horse trailing behind him, the dead town marshal wrapped in his slicker and draped over the saddle. The Last Chance was closed down, but a few bars were open and a small crowd gathered quickly as Longarm clopped down Main Street and pulled to a halt in front of the livery.

The hostler came out to greet him.

Longarm dismounted. "I got a dead man here."

"Boyd?"

Longarm nodded.

"Well, there's no place to put him."

"What do you mean?"

"The damn undertakers're all gone."

"All three?"

"Yep. And Walt and that Easterner, too."

"You mean they lit out together?"

"Nope. Walt and that Thomaris fellow rode out together, all right. But we ain't seen hide nor hair of Silas and them other two."

Longarm flipped the old man a coin and asked him to take care of his horse and Boyd's, then advised him to find a pile of horse manure on which to dump Boyd's corpse until morning. He was pulling his Winchester out of his scabbard when Tom Sanders's widow pushed through the crowd and pulled up in front of him.

"Well, Marshal, you scared them rats out of town, looks like!"

"Thank you, ma'am."

"But you ain't brought back a single kidnapped corpse. Where's my husband?"

"In heaven or hell, ma'am. But I'll be damned if I know which."

He lifted the bulging saddlebag off Boyd's horse, slung it over his shoulder, and hefting his rifle, pushed wearily through the crowd, crossed the street, and mounted the hotel's porch steps.

Jean Langly was asleep in an upholstered chair in a corner of the hotel lobby. Longarm walked over and, placing his hand on her shoulder, gently shook her awake. She reached up and took his arm.

"Custis! Thank God you're back!"

"Shh . . ." he said, leaning close. "What's wrong?"

"I discovered a body!"

Longarm pulled a chair close to hers and sat down. "Keep it down, Jean. What body did you find?"

"O'Brian's apprentice, Harry Woodward. I found him in O'Brian's vault."

"What in hell were you doing down there?"

"Never mind that. What are you going to do?"

"Stay down here. I want to take this carpetbag up to my room. I'll be right down."

"Hurry, Custis."

• • •

O'Brian's cellar and vault were lit up like a Christmas tree, the lamps hanging from the wall still burning brightly. While Jean hung back, Longarm approached the dead apprentice and looked down at his riddled body. He had been hit in the chest at what appeared to be point-blank range. He was slumped in a dark pool of his own blood, and from his person emanated the unpleasant smell of what Longarm decided was embalming fluid. And something else equally unpleasant.

He backed up and turned to Jean.

She had already explained that she had come to O'Brian's in search of the funeral director when she saw Walt Kennedy and Thomaris ride out of town. When she could not find the undertaker, she descended to the cellar and followed the lighted passageway into the lighted vaults, where she found Harry Woodward's body.

"Who would want to kill Harry?" Jean asked.

"Nobody. The way I figure it, he stumbled onto something down here and was shot as a result."

"What could he have seen? There's just these caskets."

Longarm looked past Jean at the long rows of gleaming caskets. "Yeah. That's all. Just caskets waiting for bodies."

Jean followed his gaze.

"It gives me the willies," she said.

Longarm nodded, then frowned. About ten feet down the line, he saw a casket that seemed to have an obvious defect—a neat hole drilled in the top of that mahogany lid. Something else caught his eye. The casket's lid, unlike those on both sides of it, was latched down securely. A crazy, macabre thought occurred to him. He left Jean and hurried over to the casket, snapped down the latches and flung up the lid.

Behind him, Jean gasped.

Longarm didn't feel so good himself.

Silas MacGregor, eyes bulging with terror, was lying faceup, a bullet hole in his white shirt. Longarm did not have to rest his palm against his carotid artery to know he was dead, but he did so anyway. There was no pulse and he was as cold a corpse as Longarm had ever stumbled on.

"Well, now," he muttered to Jean as he stepped back. He was thoroughly shaken. "That's one of them."

"Do you think the others . . . ?"

"It's a good guess," he replied grimly. "Look for a hole in a casket lid."

"Over there," she whispered, pointing. "The one with the gold trim."

This time Longarm found Jim Daniel. The bullet had struck him in the windpipe. His face was slack, the coffin awash in his blood. Longarm quickly slammed down the lid and, glancing further down the line of caskets, saw another neat bullet hole stamped into an otherwise immaculate, highly polished lid.

Jean crept up behind him as he lifted it.

To his astonishment he found himself looking down into O'Brian's living gaze. Like the others, his chest bore the sign of a .38 slug's neat entry, but as Longarm bent over him O'Brian managed to turn his head slightly.

"My God, man," Longarm exclaimed. "You're alive."

"Not for long," O'Brian gasped.

"Who did this?"

"Thomaris."

"Just lay still. I'll get the doc."

"No," O'Brian said. "It's too late for me. My daughter. Get her. She's with Thomaris."

"Where?"

"Denver. Clancy Street. Apartment . . . fourteen. Don't know the house number."

"Okay. Don't worry. I'll track the son of a bitch. Now you lay still and I'll go get the doc."

"Never . . . mind," O'Brian said, his voice barely audible. "Just get that bastard . . . for me."

His eyes closed. Jean leaned close, frowning down at O'Brian. Then she pulled back and looked at Longarm. There were tears on her face.

"He's gone," she said. "He lived just long enough . . ."

"Yeah . . . like he knew we'd find him. So he stayed alive just long enough to give me that address."

"I want to come, too, Custis."

"I won't stop you."

Longarm closed the coffin, then stepped back and looked back at the first one he'd opened, the one containing Silas. It was a big one, but that wasn't what he was noticing now. The glowing lantern just above the casket caused a thin, barely visible line to stand out sharply. It ran the length of the casket.

Longarm walked over and squatted to examine it more closely.

"What is it?" Jean asked.

"I'm not sure."

Longarm ran his finger along the line and found it did indeed mark a break in the coffin's side. He pulled the casket out on its wheeled platform and saw that the line completely encircled the casket. More important was the small latch he found on the back. He unlatched it and, using the open latch as a handle, lifted. With Silas's dead body resting in the casket's bed, he was able to lift the upper portion of the casket only a few inches before letting it drop.

But that one quick glimpse inside was enough.

An embalmed body was asleep in the hidden compartment hollowed out of the coffin's base.

He had found at last where the kidnapped bodies had been hidden. Dick Pratt had told him the truth when he insisted the bodies hadn't been taken anywhere. Thomaris's skill and knowledge of the coffin maker's trade had enabled him to redesign the caskets so they could contain an extra corpse. So the abducted corpses remained in each funeral home, safely tucked away inside their original casket.

In plain sight, but out of sight.

Clever.

Jean was crouching behind him.

"Did you see?" he asked her.

"Yes," she replied, her voice hushed.

"Looks like Long Tom Sanders's widow is going to be very happy."

He stood up and looked at Jean. She didn't look too good—about the same way he felt.

"Come on," he told her. "Let's get the hell out of here."

He took Jean's hand and together they fled the soul-chilling vault and hurried up the cellar stairs and out into the warm, starlit night.

Chapter 11

Longarm waited until Wallace, who also worked for Billy Vail, was in position down the hall before he leaned his head against the apartment door. He thought he heard movement inside, but he could not be certain.

He rapped softly on the door.

Nothing.

"You in there, Marylou?" he called through the door.

A small female voice close by the door on the other side whispered, "Who is it?"

"Never mind that. Are you Marylou O'Brian?"

"Yes."

"I have to see you. I've news of your father. Open up."

"My father? What about him?"

"Open the door, Marylou."

She turned the key in the lock and pulled the door open. A very young, very pretty girl with long red hair stepped back to let him in. She was dressed only in a negligee. The top buttons were unbuttoned and her cheeks were flushed. That should have warned Longarm.

He walked into the apartment, glanced quickly around, then holstered his gun and looked her over. When she saw his eyes on her childish cleavage, she quickly buttoned up the negligee.

"What about my father?" she asked.

"He's dead."

Her hand flew up to her mouth. "Dead? But . . ."

"John Thomaris killed him."

"Oh, my God!"

"Has Thomaris been here lately?"

She nodded, eyes wide, sudden tears gushing down her no-longer-flushed cheeks.

"When do you expect him back?"

"Don't sweat it, Marshal," a harsh male voice barked from a doorway to his right. "I'm already here."

Barefoot, Thomaris was wearing only his trousers. His .38 leveled on Longarm, he strode into the room and kicked the apartment door shut. Then he turned the key in the lock and glanced at Marylou.

"This son of a bitch is lying," he told her. "I didn't have nothin' to do with your pa's death."

"Then he *is* dead," she cried, "and you knew it."

"It was an accident."

Longarm spoke up then. "What Thomaris did, Marylou, was make your father get into one of his own caskets. Then he shot him through the lid. Your father lived long enough to give me this address."

The girl looked at Thomaris in wide-eyed shock. She knew Thomaris well enough to believe without question Longarm's account of her father's death. "You bastard," she hissed.

Thomaris shrugged. "Have it your way, Marylou. But I'm tellin' you, this lawman is lying through his teeth."

"He ain't lyin'!" Marylou flung at him. "You killed my pa!"

His patience gone, Thomaris stepped closer and slapped Marylou. "Shut up!" he barked meanly. "Just shut up, you fool kid. You hated your old man and that town. Now you're rid of both. You should be grateful."

She took a step back from him, her hand up to her stinging cheek.

That was when Wallace—his shoulder and head down—came through the door like a runaway locomotive, pieces of the door clinging to him as he sprawled on the carpet. Thomaris spun to fire on him. Longarm flung himself upon him and twisted the gun out of his grasp. When it hit the floor, he kicked it into a corner, then drove Thomaris back against the wall, burying his fist into the man's gut so deep, he was sure he had bent the son of a bitch's backbone. With a gasp, Thomaris sagged all the way to the floor—in no condition to continue the battle.

As Longarm stepped back two thunderous detonations filled the room and he saw first one and then another slug stamp a hole in Thomaris's naked chest. A third shot caught the man in his left eye. Longarm swung about and saw Marylou's face twisted into a mindless rage as she continued to aim down at her dead lover.

"Give me that gun," Longarm commanded, stepping toward her.

Instead, she swung it up to cover him and Wallace.

"March into the closet," she told them, nodding at a clothes closet beside the entry.

Both men hesitated.

Like a small child stamping her foot, Marylou fired a round into the floor at their feet. Neither one of them offered any further argument as they marched into the closet. Marylou slammed the door shut behind them and turned the key in the lock. A few moments later they heard her leaving. As soon as the apartment door closed behind her both men hurled themselves at the closet door. It took three attempts, but at last the door's panels splintered and the two men stumbled out. With drawn guns, they charged out of the apartment and headed down the stairs.

Halfway down the second flight they halted.

They could hear Jean Langly in the landing at the foot of the stairs. She was talking to Marylou.

"Why, I haven't seen you in so long, Marylou!" Jean cried.

"Yeah, it's real nice seeing you again," Marylou said.

"My, you sure are loaded down there. What *do* you have in those carpetbags? Do you need any help?"

"I don't need no help, Jean. I'm all right. Honest. I got to go now."

"No, you don't, Marylou."

The two men heard the sounds of a short struggle, followed by the sharp crack of a palm striking a cheek.

"And I'll just take this here gun," they heard Jean say. "You might hurt yourself."

Immediately there came the sound of Marylou's ragged sobs. It was such a storm, it seemed to fill the entire stairwell. Longarm and Wallace bolted on down the stairs. When they reached the second-floor landing, they peered over the railing and saw Marylou huddled on the bottom step, crying as if her heart would break, while Jean poked through the three large carpetbags.

When Jean saw them coming down the stairs toward her, she reached into one of the carpetbags and held up a fistful of bank notes.

"Here's the money!" she told them.

Wallace held up. "Maybe you better be the one to tell her what Marylou just done to Thomaris back there."

In a hideaway booth in the Windsor Hotel's lounge, where some privileged women were allowed to accompany their male companions, Longarm took a sip of his beer and lit a cheroot, then leaned back to gaze on Jean Langly. She had ordered a glass of sarsaparilla. He was seriously considering asking her to stay on in the Mile High City—for another week, at least.

"Once I saw her carrying those carpetbags," Jean was saying, "I knew what was up. But if I'd known she had just shot Thomaris, I'm sure I would not have been so brave."

"Sure you would've," he said, reaching over and taking her hand. "You are a very brave woman. All the same, I'm not so happy that you disobeyed my orders."

She smiled and tipped her head, amused. "Standing in that doorway across the street was just as dangerous, Custis. Maybe more so. Do you have any idea how many men stopped, doffed their hats, and asked my price?"

Longarm smiled. "I never thought of that."

"It was *not* a very nice neighborhood for a woman to be seen loitering in a dark doorway."

Longarm chuckled. "Maybe not. But I can understand why you would draw a man's attention."

Jean considered that for a moment, then shrugged. "It is not the kind of attention I prefer to draw, Custis—and the men were no prize packages, I can assure you."

To that Longarm had no response.

"Tell me, Custis," she said, serious all of a sudden. "What will happen to Marylou?"

"She might get off with probation or a short stretch in prison. After all, the man she killed did have the ransom money in his possession—the marked bills prove that without question. And he not only did away with Marylou's father, but a small army besides. Only God knows where he left Walt Kennedy's ventilated body. My guess is the vultures are feeding on it right now somewhere between here and Golden."

"What a terrible man," Jean said softly, shuddering.

"In our statements, Wallace and I indicated we were in a desperate struggle with Thomaris when Marylou fired on him—that it was her quick action that saved us."

"But that's not true, is it?"

"Not entirely. But it's close enough."

Jean thought that over for a few minutes, then shrugged. "I guess you're right. Punishing Marylou any further wouldn't accomplish anything. She's been through enough already."

"My thoughts exactly."

They sat for a while in silence, letting the memories of Golden and its crowded vaults slip away from them, like the cold mists of an unpleasant night. After a few moments Jean lifted the glass of sarsaparilla to her lips and took a sip.

"That was a lovely dinner, Custis."

"There's plenty more where that came from. Stay around awhile, Jean. Brighten up the Mile High City."

"Sounds nice, Custis. But I can't. I really must get back to New York."

"To pick up your reward."

"*If* what we both think is true and I find Alexander Stewart's body hidden somewhere inside the family vault—just where no one would think to look for it."

"We might be wrong."

She made a face. "You're such a spoilsport."

He grinned. "It'll be there. I'm sure of it."

"That's much better, Custis."

Glancing up, Longarm saw Billy Vail approaching. On his arm was Mrs. Sanders, the poor little old widow woman whose shotgun blast had been the opening salvo in the mayhem that all the Eastern papers were now writing up.

"May we join you?" Billy asked.

"Come right ahead," said Longarm, nodding a greeting to the widow as he spoke. "We'd be delighted."

Once Billy and his guest were seated in the booth and their drinks had been brought to them, Billy pulled his schooner of beer closer and got right to the point.

"The town of Golden is in a shambles, Longarm."

"Tell me something I don't know, chief."

"So I got a proposition for you."

Longarm winked at Jean. "Shoot," he said.

"I've decided to appoint you temporary town marshal—until Golden's town council can come up with an honest town marshal and some deputies to take over."

"Just lawmen you're looking for? You'll also need a new crew of undertakers, I'm thinking."

"Morticians," Mrs. Sanders corrected sharply. She took a sip of her beer. "They don't like to be called undertakers."

"Sorry," Longarm told her.

"Right now, Custis," Vail said, brushing aside the widow's interruption, "it's law we need, not undertakers. What do you say?"

"Sorry, chief."

"Now, dammit, don't be so quick to say no. You can do it. I've already cleared it with Washington."

"I got other plans. And I've already cleared it with the third-floor bureaucracy. I'm leaving on my vacation tomorrow."

"Vacation? Tomorrow?" Vail almost knocked over his beer. "You can't!"

"I told you. It's already been okayed."

"Where the hell you goin'?"

"New York City—to help Jean here find a very old corpse."

Jean laughed, delighted.

"My God, Longarm. Ain't you through with poking around graves yet?"

"Not with such a lovely companion."

Longarm dropped enough coins to cover his and Vail's tab, then left the booth with Jean before Vail had an apoplectic fit.

In bed not much later, Longarm propped himself up on his elbow and gazed at the snowy hills and dark, lush valleys of Jean's long figure.

"Was that better?"

She laughed softly. "I always knew it wasn't lack of will," she told him. "It's just that you were always so tired when I happened along. And then there were so many widows in Golden. I didn't stand a chance."

Longarm lay back down and stared up at the ceiling. He was thinking of Eileen Turnbill, and he didn't want to.

Jean poked him gently. "Tell me," she said. "Suppose I refused to let you accompany me back to New York."

"Now, why would you do a thing like that?"

"Because I think all you want is half of that reward, not me."

"You're wrong."

"You don't want half the reward?"

"I want half of the reward *and* you."

She laughed and snuggled closer.

"Done," she said.